W.Y. BOYD

A RENDEZVOUS with DEATH

ELTON-WOLF PUBLISHING

A RENDEZVOUS with DEATH

Cover design by David Marty
Text design by Jeanne Hendrickson

Published by Elton-Wolf Publishing
Seattle, Washington

This is a work of fiction. Names, characters, places, and incidents are either the product of the author's imagination or are used fictitiously, and any resemblance to actual persons, living or dead, business establishments, events, or locales is entirely coincidental.

ISBN: 1-58619-046-6
Library of Congress Catalog Number: 2003102754
07 06 05 04 03   1 2 3 4 5

First Edition June 2003
Printed in the United States

ELTON-WOLF PUBLISHING
2505 Second Avenue Suite 515 Seattle, Washington 98121
Tel 206.748.0345 Fax 206.748.0343
www.elton-wolf.com info@elton-wolf.com
Seattle • Los Angeles

To all American combat infantry
past and present
★

PREFACE

———◆———

E xcept for the murders, all the events related in *A Rendezvous With Death* are based on actual historical fact. The first sequence describes a typical infantry combat situation. Associated with this was Patton's Fifth Infantry Division crossing the Rhine at Oppenheim on March 22, 1945. The dash to Hechingen and its purpose is also factual, although slightly altered for the sake of the continuity of the story. All this has been accepted without question by my readers.

However, several of them have told me they find it difficult to believe that the U.S. Army would send in less than thirty infantrymen to hold a town against five hundred SS officer candidates, even though a river separated them. The strange thing is that this incident is based on an actual situation in which I was personally involved. Those of you who have read *The Gentle Infantryman* know I was in an infantry antitank mine platoon. By the time we got to the Main River, there weren't many mines, so we filled in as riflemen.

Preparing for the assault on Wurzburg, we were suddenly pulled out of line and told we were going back to the rear to guard a German hospital. Great! Except that at the outskirts of the town on the Main, we learned that our primary mission would be to keep some five hundred elite SS officer candidates on the other side of the river from crossing and raising hell in the American rear. Our platoon consisted of eighteen men including two drivers. An antitank gun from our third platoon joined us, with eight men including a driver and a medic. (Most infantry outfits, which had been in combat for any length of time, were operating at about half strength—if they were lucky.) So there we were: twenty-six men against five hundred SS, right off the Russian front. To keep this short, the Germans mortared the hell out of us and we shot back with our one machine gun and our rifles. The antitank gun shot a couple of enemy landing craft out of the water. The battle for the town was fierce. On the third day, some units from the famous Rainbow Division, which had crossed at Wurzburg, arrived on the east bank of the Main and wiped out the SS.

Under certain circumstances, it was not unusual for the U.S. Army to order small units of infantry to fight far superior enemy forces. This also happened to my company during the Battle of the Bulge. The orders were "to hold at all costs" even though outnumbered by about twenty to one. We held.

This shows that truth is harder to believe than fiction, which is the reason I always fictionalize my World War II novels.

A RENDEZVOUS with DEATH

1

In the predawn darkness of March 21, 1945, at 0600 hours, some forty assault boats belonging to Task Force Coleman slipped quietly away from the western bank of the Rhine and disappeared into the gloom. Crouched low, the soldiers of the second wave could barely make out the shadows of the boats ahead of them as they melted into the light mist. The muffled throb of the boats' engines was the only sound disturbing the silence that lay like a blanket across the black waters.

Kneeling in the bow of one of the last boats, Second Lieutenant Charles Donnelly, commander of an antitank platoon, now down to one gun, could feel his heart pounding. He prayed that the darkness would last forever and that the fog would never lift. Until this moment, Charles Donnelly had always looked forward to the dawn. But now, as he saw the faint grey in the eastern sky, he felt only dread. Ahead, on the Nazi-held east bank of the river, lay the enemy. Somewhere amidst the seemingly peaceful, rural landscape lurked armies of German soldiers waiting to kill him. Behind lay the safety of the American forces that had swept through Europe. Charles, six feet tall, had a face with straight features and, to his chagrin and dismay, prematurely grey hair. His friends told him his grey hair and young face made him irresistible to the ladies, but he refused to believe it. After all, even though they seemed to enjoy his company, he hadn't noticed any ladies exactly throwing themselves at him.

Charles's father was a federal judge. He had urged Charles to get a commission in Naval Intelligence. Charles had replied, "No, sir. If I have to go to war, then, dammit, I'm going to war. I'm not going to sit behind a desk for the duration." He could tell his father was proud of him for his decision but was apprehensive, too. He loved his father but saw little of him, and he knew his father loved him. He just wished they knew how to communicate better with each other.

"We're getting close," one of his soldiers whispered behind him. Donnelly nodded in the dark. He could feel the tension of his men packed closely around him in the small landing craft, which resembled nothing more than a huge steel box with a ramp on the front that would be lowered to allow the troops and vehicles to disembark. He scanned the approaching bank. He was just as frightened as his troops, but as their leader he could not show it. The steel landing boat held the antitank gun, a Jeep and eight men. Charles heard the splashing of water against the ramp of the boat as it moved slowly toward the eastern shore. Were hostile eyes watching their every move? He understood only too well that at any moment a blast of enemy fire could obliterate his boat and everybody in it.

As everybody knew, one bridgehead had already been established on the Rhine, further north at Remagan, when the Ludendorf Bridge had been captured on March 7th by Omar Bradley's First Army. In a political move, orders had been given to stay put until the British made the first official river crossing of the Rhineland campaign. That left Patton chomping at the bit to get across, and he had made no secret of it. Now he was taking things into his own hands. That night at ten o'clock, his Fifth Infantry Division would cross the Rhine at Oppenheim and establish a bridgehead. He would refer to the operation as "a patrol in force," but once the Third Army was successfully across, no one would question Patton, and the history books would show who the real victors were. To assure success, Patton had chosen Colonel Larry Coleman, Donnelly's regimental commander, to lead a small force across the river north of Oppenheim. Task Force

Coleman was a decoy which Patton hoped would turn the German attention away from Oppenheim. Once Coleman was across, the enemy would send whatever units they had in the area to fight the task force, giving Patton a chance to cross unchallenged.

After Patton divulged the plan to Colonel Coleman, Coleman had briefed the officers who would make the diversionary crossing.

Donnelly pulled his woolen scarf tighter around his neck. Twenty-five was too young to die. There were still so many things that he wanted to do... finish law school... visit the Grand Canyon... celebrate his father's tenth anniversary as a federal judge... see his younger brother graduate from college... he hoped his brother, David, would be all right. He'd been drafted during his freshman year at Harvard and was already taking infantry basic training.

Donnelly felt the flat bow of the boat bump into the muddy bank of the river and the next instant he was up and jumping onto land. He could see the mist still hanging over the river like steam from a hot bath. Though he knew that there were more boats hidden in the mists behind him, he saw nothing—heard only the rushing river. For a moment he breathed a sigh of relief. Perhaps his own boat had been as silent. He saw through the diminishing mist that ahead of him was a line of grass, and he could make out bushes and pine trees. There was no sound of gunfire. No sound at all. With his fears at least briefly laid to rest, he began to take in the lay of the land.

As Donnelly surveyed his surroundings, his sergeant, Bull Kelly, supervised the men. Quickly, they unloaded the Jeep and hooked up the antitank gun, commonly known as a 57 because it fired a 57 mm shell. Donnelly had requested Kelly, though they were an unlikely pair—tall, lean Charles, the privileged Yale law student, and Kelly, the son of a New York Irish cop, stocky and barrel-chested with the look of an angry bulldog—but they had become good friends, and Charles knew he could rely on Bull to lead the men. They had only one gun of their three-gun platoon, but Charles hoped it would be enough.

He jumped behind the steering wheel of the Jeep, and with four other soldiers, including Bull in the Jeep and three others mounted on the gun, he started up the hill towards the open field to find the rifle companies.

The rutted field rose up from the riverbank toward the hills beyond. Dark forests spread out like wings on both sides of the field. Charles crested the hill and stopped. To his right a dilapidated farmhouse stood on the highest ground for miles around. From here, Charles could just see the last of the rifle companies making their way across a small meadow into the woods below. Beyond the woods he could see more farmland, and in the far distance, a town. But everything was dead quiet, not a trace of the Jerries. Still, Charles knew from his last encounter with the enemy just how quickly this could change.

He continued driving into the woods, pulling the antitank gun towards the left flank of the rifle companies. Once he found a suitable spot, Bull and the men positioned it to cover the road that any panzers who knew their business would use. A 57 mm antitank gun could not penetrate the thick frontal armor of a German Tiger tank. A shot in the side or rear could do the job sometimes, or a hit on the treads could stop the Tiger's forward motion. If a gunner were really good, he could fire so his shell would hit just in front of the Tiger and ricochet into its soft underside, provided the ground was hard. Donnelly knew he'd have to depend on the rifles of the battalion to support him. The Jerries wouldn't send in their tanks without infantry because they'd be unprotected from enemy infantry who could get close enough to slaughter them with bazookas.

After concealing the gun in the thick pine woods, Donnelly and Bull turned their attention to the three extra men they'd managed to fit onto the boat in addition to the gun crew.

"I think I ought to take them into the woods back the way we came," Donnelly said quietly.

Bull nodded. "You'll be able to see better from there and you can add your firepower to cover the gun against an infantry attack."

Both knew that it was smarter for them to separate. If either man was put out of action, the other could handle the gun squad. "Be careful," Donnelly said, knowing that the gun would be a prime target.

Bull nodded. "Don't worry about me, sir. Just get going. See you in Berlin."

"See you in Berlin," responded Charles and waved farewell.

Donnelly took his men into the trees and found a place from which they could see the rifle companies crouched silently in their recently-dug foxholes, waiting. Their positions were perfect to defend the gun and men against any German attack.

Charles was turning back towards the pines, when the *crack!* of a German 88 mm shell split the air. He dove to the ground and waited. An awesome, all-purpose weapon, the 88 was an anti-aircraft, anti-personnel, and deadly antitank gun. Its velocity was so fast, the Americans heard the shell's explosion before hearing it zip through the air. Charles remembered the story of Eisenhower asking a tank man if the German 88 shell could penetrate an American tank's armor. The man had replied, "Oh, no sir! It just goes in one side and comes out the other." Recalling the story always made Charles smile.

In the silence that followed the first single blast of the 88 gun, Charles looked up to see where the shot had come from. What he saw almost made his heart stop. Four Tiger tanks crawled down the road like a column of giant insects silhouetted against the rising sun.

The Tigers fired at the Americans with devastating accuracy. 88 shells exploded around all the battalion positions. Donnelly could hear men screaming for medics. All he could do was lie on the damp ground, paralyzed with fear as shells blew up all around him. Donnelly saw infantry behind the Tigers, a full-scale attack.

Suddenly Charles heard the unmistakable bang of the antitank gun. Bull was firing back at the tanks. Charles raised himself on all fours. Across the field, a knocked-out Tiger tank blazed on the road, sending up billows of black smoke. Atta boy, Bull, thought Donnelly. Now get outta there! Through the trees, he saw Kelly's gun crew start to roll the 57 to another position before the other Tigers spotted it.

But they were too late. An 88 shell landed less than ten feet from the gun, and shrapnel mowed down Bull and his gun crew. The gun remained forlorn and unmanned. Helplessly, Donnelly observed the slain men, praying for even one of them to move, to moan, to show the slightest sign of life. But there was none.

The gun sat alone and silent at the edge of the woods, its flash shield perforated by shrapnel. For the first time since the attack began, Charles Donnelly forced himself to think. Already he could see the three remaining tanks maneuvering around the knocked-out tank and heading into the field toward the American line, searching for the gun they were hoping they had destroyed. Getting to his feet, Donnelly called to his men, "Novak! Cousins! Russo! Let's go!"

They raced across the battlefield, reaching the gun within seconds. "Let's move it over there!" Donnelly screamed, pointing to another grove of trees about fifty feet to the right. Running, pulling, gasping for breath, the men hauled their gun to a new position between two tall stands of trees. Donnelly immediately took aim. With his first shot, he knocked out one of the three remaining Tigers. "Bull's eye!" he breathed. He heard his men let the pent-up air out of their lungs.

Instantly he saw another Tiger's turret swivel, seeking him out. The panzer's gun barrel stopped moving, ominously pointed directly at the four soldiers manning the gun.

Charles didn't wait. He pulled the firing bar, hard. Then, up and off. No time to look.

"Go, go, go!" he screamed to his men. If he had missed the tank, they would be dead. Acting as gunner was not his usual function as the leader of a platoon, so as he went, Donnelly kept going over in his mind the skills of aiming and firing that he had learned so well in his training.

As they raced to another position, pulling the gun as fast as they ran, Donnelly thought, three Tigers down, one to go. An 88 exploded in front and to the right of him. As Donnelly threw himself to the ground, he felt a sting on his forehead. But he was up quickly, guiding the gun through the woods again, then leaning into the gunner's cradle. The German infantry was closer to the American line now, firing as they advanced. But the machine guns and rifles of the Third Battalion were slowing their progress.

The remaining Tiger charged towards the gun, its 88 aimed at Donnelly's gun crew. If he hesitated even a second, they would all be dead. Then, suddenly he couldn't see. Blood poured into his eyes from the wound across his forehead. He wiped his eyes and his hand came away red and sticky. But he could now see.

He pulled hard at the firing bar, his right eye glued to the gun sight. He saw his shell hit the Tiger's turret, just below its gun barrel, then ricochet off in a ball of fire. It bounced a couple of times in the field before it came to rest.

He aimed his next shot straight at the muzzle of the 88. His last armor-piercing shell had jarred the German tankmen and thrown them off balance. But they wouldn't stay that way long. He had one chance left. A 57 mm shell could never penetrate the frontal armor of a Tiger tank, so he would try to knock the tank's gun out of alignment. He pulled the firing bar.

Donnelly saw his second shot hit the Tiger's barrel, striking sparks. He got up to help pull the gun away again—it was now or never—they had to change position before the tank crew recovered. As he got to his feet and started to tug at the gun, he heard a cheer from the woods.

"Lieutenant, look!" Russo pointed. The Tiger's turret hung lopsided, its gun barrel wrenched out of line and pointing toward the ground. The tank sat in the field, feeble and impotent.

Donnelly took his hand off the gun and leaned into the gunner's cradle. He aimed at the right tread of the tank and pulled the bar. He had learned the hard way this past winter: Even if it couldn't shoot its 88, the driver might start that panzer up again and come charging at them, machine guns blazing. The shell hit the tread squarely, breaking it in two. Now the tank sat completely helpless. Donnelly sank to the ground both relieved and exhausted. His helmet lay under the tree where he had first been hit.

"You're hit bad, Lieutenant," Cousins said, helping Donnelly to his feet.

Just then, the Tiger tank's turret top opened.

"They're coming out," Russo whispered. A hand reached up from the turret, but a hail of fire from the American battalion's riflemen greeted the effort, and the hand instantly disappeared. A bazooka team ran forward, preparing to fire.

"No!" Donnelly shouted. He ran towards them waving his arms. "Wait! Wait! Those are my prisoners! Hold off!"

The men looked at Donnelly in confusion.

"Wait!" he shouted again.

Charles stared at the iron monster that, only moments ago, had been so lethal. He pointed his Tommy gun at the turret.

"*Kommen sie hier! Kommen sie hier! Mit der hand am kopf!*" he shouted awkwardly.

No response.

Again he shouted for the tank crew to come out with their hands on their heads. Still nothing. The last shots had crackled across the field, and now there was only black smoke billowing into the air from the knocked out tanks—and a heavy silence.

Suddenly one of the tank's machine gun barrels moved. Donnelly's instincts kicked in, causing him to throw himself to the ground just as the gun fired. Bullets stitched a straight row of dust spots in front of him, kicking dirt into his wound and hair. The Germans in the Tiger had gotten one of their small machine guns working and now sprayed the field.

When the firing stopped, Donnelly rose slightly to signal the bazooka-men to go get the bastards, but they were already aiming at the tank. A split second later the armor-piercing rocket blasted into the Tiger's side. A ring of white smoke drifted out the open turret. The smell of death floated across the battlefield.

Charles sighed wearily. Although it seemed an eternity, he knew the entire action had lasted only a matter of minutes. The final wave of boats was probably still making the crossing. Heavy firing could be heard farther up the river from the few platoons already in First Battalion position, which meant they were now under attack. Charles wondered if the enemy had sent in tanks to assault the First Battalion, or just infantry. His heart sank. He couldn't fight off another column of Tiger tanks; he just didn't have it in him. His legs were shaking so badly he could hardly stand. He stumbled and fell to his knees.

Cousins grabbed his arm. "We're getting you to the aid station, Lieutenant."

"No, I have to report to the colonel. We have no communications lines and if I don't tell him, he won't know we were able to repulse the panzers."

His men nodded reluctantly.

"Just let me sit here and catch my wind a minute." Charles really was exhausted. To steady his nerves, he tried to turn his thoughts to more pleasant times. May in 1942. After graduating from Yale, he'd managed to get in a year of law school. Even though his family lived in Chicago, they spent their summers on Nantucket Island off Cape Cod. It was a long trip, the train ride from Chicago to Boston, then to Woods Hole and the ferry, which made a stop at Martha's Vineyard on the way to Nantucket. The ride from Nantucket town across the island to Siasconset, always called "Sconset," was short. That summer everybody drank "sea breezes"—gin and grapefruit juice. Although not a great drinker, Charles enjoyed one or two before dinner. He smiled at the memory.

He continued to distract himself by reliving his days on the beach sunning himself and swimming. He'd flirt with the girls, of which there were many that summer, but he took a particular liking to Muffy, a statuesque blond from New Jersey. After dinner parties, which took place every evening, he and Muffy would go somewhere out of the way. They'd kiss passionately and caress each other, but, despite Charles's best efforts, it never got any further than that. The night before Charles left for the army, he implored Muffy to let him make love to her, but to no avail. She told him she was a virgin and would never give in unless he married her. In his state of mind, he said, "Yes, yes. Of course." But she'd been too smart to believe him.

Every time he thought of that June, Charles felt on top of the world. He had been a very happy young man. Then, he reported for induction into the Army of the United States.

2

On March 21, 1945, at 0900 hours, Colonel Lawrence Coleman stepped out onto the sagging porch of the deserted farmhouse where he had set up his Task Force Coleman command post. Situated on the high ground a half mile inland from the river, the house provided a good view of the area, though the small forest below blocked the Third Battalion positions where the morning's battle raged. Coleman could see smoke rising from the battlefield. The firing of 88s had stopped; so had the antitank gun. The bulk of the gunfire now came from further upriver, where First Battalion was dug in.

Coleman jumped down off the porch onto the grass. A West Pointer and full colonel at thirty-eight, Coleman was a bachelor. Tall, with angular features on his reddish-brown face and a full head of brown hair, he could be considered craggily handsome. As a senior officer, he was considered resolute and brilliant by his peers and was well liked by his men. Comfortable in command, he maintained an informal relationship with his subordinates that a less competent officer would never permit for fear of losing their respect or obedience.

Coleman strode impatiently toward the hill, waiting for his communications section to get set up. Why was it taking so long to string a few wires? And where the hell was Lou? He should have reported back already. Lou Ames, twenty years old and his sister's only child, was like a son to him. He had even assigned Lou to his own staff to make sure the boy stayed out of trouble.

Climbing up onto an old stone wall, Coleman looked out through his binoculars. The sun had risen high over the distant hills, and the grey dawn had given way to scattered clouds. His bridgehead had been secured. An aid station was already set up near the landing site, and Coleman could see his men carrying the wounded and the dead back to the riverbank.

Then he caught sight of Charles Donnelly limping towards him. Blood dripped from Donnelly's forehead and covered most of the front of his shirt and field jacket. When he reached his commander, he brushed his right hand across the cleft in his helmet in what was supposed to pass as a salute.

"I heard the firing," said Coleman. "Sounded like you were attacked by several Tiger tanks and fought back."

"Yes, sir. Four Tigers. Kelly got the first one, but one of the others got him. Our gun crew was knocked out. All gone. I took over with my three men and we got the rest of the Tigers. It was touch and go, though, sir. The last one almost got us, hit me in the head with a piece of shrapnel."

"Why haven't you had that gash on your forehead attended to?"

"Sir, I thought I should report to you first."

"You did right, Charles. You're a damned good man, and I'm going to remember that. Those Tigers could've thrown us back into the Rhine. Now, go straight to the aid station, then report back."

As Donnelly started to leave, Coleman barked, "Why are you limping? I thought you got hit in the head."

Charles smiled as he said, "I thought limping was obligatory whenever you got hit, sir."

Coleman had to laugh. "Get out of here, you damned goldbrick."

Actually, Donnelly had a knee badly sprained playing college football, and he had wrenched it during the panzer attack.

An hour later Buddy Marks, Coleman's closest aide, came lumbering across the field to join him on the edge of the hill. At six foot four and two hundred fifty pounds, he might at first appear a formidable foe, but Buddy was clearly a simple, good-hearted soul. His face was plain and pallid, almost ugly except for his engaging smile and curly hair. But he was not bright, and some wondered why Coleman had chosen the slow-witted officer as his aide, but to Coleman there had never been a question. Marks had grown up in the army, and his father, a four-star general, had instilled in his awkward son three things that, to Coleman's thinking, made him a first-class soldier: Duty, Honor, and Country. Marks might not be a genius, but he was loyal to the bone and would never question a command.

Marks arrived at the bottom of the stone wall, red-faced and out of breath. "Sir..." he panted.

"What news?" the colonel asked impatiently.

"Lieutenant Donnelly, sir…. He took out four tanks. The men said he was hit, sir. Most of his crew killed, including Sergeant Kelly."

Coleman nodded. "I know. I saw Charles. Still, every time my men get killed, I die a little." His voice carried a note of sadness. "But four tanks! Good God! I wonder how badly Donnelly was really hit."

"Somebody said he was bleeding to death, sir."

Worried, Coleman said, "Do me a favor, Buddy. Go to the aid station and find out how hurt Donnelly really is. Then get back here on the double. Okay?"

"Yes, sir," replied Buddy hesitantly, not at all sure where the aid station was.

Coleman had just stepped back inside the command post when he heard a series of huge explosions. Before he could get back outside to find out what had happened, Major Ramon Gonzalez-Rivera, his executive officer, came rushing in.

"Colonel, something's blowing up all over the right flank. Lieutenant Sauter's sector."

Coleman nodded. "It sounds like trouble. Where's St. John?" Until he got his communications set up, Coleman would have to use his officers as messengers to keep him advised of the situation.

"He's on his way up from the river," said Gonzalez-Rivera. "He went down to make sure we all got across."

"Damn. I need him to check Sauter's sector," Coleman said anxiously. A thought occurred to him. His nephew, Lou, was in the same area as Sauter's platoon. And he had not reported back.

Just then, Lieutenant John St. John sauntered into the command post. He took off his helmet. "Greetings," he said. "Lovely day for a war, eh?" St. John had the relaxed air of someone for whom everything had come easily. He was the intelligence and reconnaissance officer of the regiment and was slim and, at six feet tall, looked almost skinny. He had fine straight blond hair, already thinning slightly, and his nose short, mouth full, and a cleft chin, which gave his other features their strong character. The man was self-assured. "I'm going to leave you gentlemen for a few minutes. Saw something I want to check out," he said nonchalantly.

"Before you do, Johnny, I want you to find out what's going on over on our right flank, Sauter's sector."

"Sounded like a minefield going off," said St. John. He opened his canteen and took a long drink of water.

Coleman looked worried. "Get over there right away and find out exactly what's going on. Lou should be around there somewhere. If you find him, tell him to get his butt back here immediately. We'll have our radios working in a few minutes."

St. John nodded.

"Move it," Coleman growled.

Major Gonzalez-Rivera, a Venezuelan turned American who had recently joined the regiment, had brought up the rear of the assault boats crossing the Rhine that morning. He felt exhilarated. He'd expected to be afraid and to show it. If he had, he was sure the men would have made fun of him and he couldn't have stood that. No! Never. But he hadn't been afraid. He focused his attention on getting as many men and supplies as possible across the Rhine before the Germans cut them off. All those enemy bullets and shells were an annoyance, but nothing more. To the young major, crossing the Rhine was a problem like any other; it took skill and brains and he had plenty of both.

Now he waited until the other men had left the room then turned to the colonel and spoke carefully. "Sir, I have some good news for you." He had been making corrections to the papers on his clipboard, and now he handed the board to Colonel Coleman.

Coleman studied the figures. "Lord! That's twice as much stuff as I thought we would be able to get over. You're very good."

"I like to think so, sir."

"You're a damned genius, Ramon. Now, if you can get this damned radio set-up to work, I'll give you a medal."

"That's not insurmountable," said Ramon, smiling. "First, I'll go check on the wire crews, then get the walkie-talkies to give clear signals."

Two platoons from "B" Company had made the crossing with their captain, a tough up-from-the-ranks former sergeant named Paul Turner. They'd dug their foxholes alongside a shallow creek that emptied into the Rhine. They fought off an enemy attack almost at once. The enemy probe had been weak, and most of the Germans had retired, leaving a dozen or so bodies strewn along the bank or in the water of the creek.

A small and wiry man, Paul Turner had a hooked nose and a nasty disposition. On occasion his fellow officers referred to him as "Ferret Face" and the resemblance wasn't too far off. His eyes gleamed with the shrewdness and cunning his nickname implied. This was a man who missed nothing and anticipated everything.

Captain Turner felt restless. He had heard heavy firing in the Third Battalion's area; heard the 88s hitting the Americans and the 57 shooting back at the panzers. He'd heard mines exploding in Sauter's sector and prayed that Sauter and his men had been out of the way when the mines blew. He fidgeted. Until he got in radio contact with the regiment, he couldn't find out what was going on. Only rough static crackled over his radio. What the hell was going on at headquarters?

He turned to Joe Ainsley, his young executive officer from Cleveland, and said, "Take over for me. I'm gonna do me a little recon and find out what's going on around here."

Once, Lieutenant St. John commanded a regulation Intelligence and Reconnaissance Platoon, but after most of his men were killed or wounded, he went to the top G-2 officers of the Third Army and obtained permission to operate alone—a platoon in name only. For reasons unknown to his comrades, G-2 agreed as long as he continued to function as I & R officer. At that stage of the war, a platoon wasn't necessary as long as there was one good man to handle its functions capably. He also received a promotion to captain.

St. John now made his way towards an open field that had been recently plowed by artillery shells and exploding mines. Far to his left, he could see the silhouettes of four Tiger tanks. Two were still sending up billows of black smoke; the other two sat motionless, simply knocked out. He moved cautiously, low to the ground, from bush to tree to stone wall. When he reached a ditch close to the ravaged field, he surveyed his front. Hank Sauter's platoon had been blown to pieces. St. John peered out at the landscape of colors: the bright green of sprouting grass, the blackened splotches where artillery shells and mines had exploded and the remains of Sauter's soldiers—red, white, purple, olive-drab—just colors, strewn over a small area of the field. Nothing moved. Not one man was left alive. St. John could feel the bile rising from his stomach, catching in his throat. In the cover of the ditch, he squatted and tried to crank the field telephone. He waited. Nothing. Then he tried again and got some crackling. At least somebody was trying to get the thing to work.

While he waited, he assessed the situation. Clearly, there had been no Germans around to observe what happened to Hank

Sauter's men. In all likelihood, a couple of stray artillery shells had fallen short of their intended targets and had detonated all the mines in the field just as Sauter's platoon crossed it. St. John wondered how much time he had before the Germans realized that there was nothing to stop them from launching a flanking attack straight across this field into the American rear.

He poked his head over the top of the ditch again. On the far side of the field something moved. He stayed very still. Now he saw them. Germans were approaching, cautiously probing to see what had happened and whether the area was defended. He had to do something quickly or there would soon be enemy battalions pouring through that field right into the rear of Coleman's Task Force. He put his Tommy gun to his shoulder, steadied it, and when the first German started to move from one hole to another, he squeezed the trigger and saw the German dive for cover. Now they would think the area was defended. He hunched down again in the ditch and cranked the box, praying that it was working. "St. John to C.P. Sauter's wiped out. Jerries probing. Send me some help quick or it'll be too late."

There was silence on the other end. St. John hoped he'd been heard, but he couldn't be sure. He was about to try again when a voice came through the box. "We hear you. Help on the way from Turner. They'll approach from southwest. Repeat, they'll approach from the southwest."

"Roger, out." Southwest meant from his rear. That was good. And he was glad it was Turner. The man knew his business. Suddenly the Germans in the field began firing back. He heard burp guns and rifles. As he stuck his head up for a quick look he saw a single American G.I. heading straight for the ditch. St. John gave him cover, firing at the Germans, who stopped shooting and went to ground. His clip emptied, he threw it away and pulled another from his field jacket pocket and jammed it into the Thompson. Pulling back the bolt he let it slide forward to ram a .45 cartridge into the chamber.

The G.I. threw himself into the ditch head first and lay panting. It was Lieutenant Lou Ames, Coleman's nephew.

"What the hell is going on here?" Ames asked breathlessly.

"What does it look like? Sauter got wiped out in a minefield."

"My uncle sent me out to scout the right flank. He said it would be quiet."

"Yeah, he said I might run into you. And I'm damned glad I did," said John. "You can help me hold off these Krauts until help comes."

"I'd like to, Johnny," Ames whined, "but my orders are to reconnoiter Sauter's sector and report back to the colonel."

"Bullshit! Coleman already knows about Sauter. I'm in radio contact."

"Sorry Johnny, but those are my orders."

"Stay and help me, for God's sake!" St. John's voice betrayed his desperation. He couldn't believe Ames would even consider leaving him alone in a situation like this. St. John reached out to grab Ames by his field jacket, but Lou slipped out of reach.

As Ames scampered off to the rear, St. John raised his Tommy gun and aimed at Ames's back. He held the gun there for a long second. Then, slowly, almost reluctantly, he lowered it. "You cowardly son of a bitch," he whispered.

Charles sat slumped on the floor of the aid station, waiting for one of the medics to dress his wounds. Already the place was full of wounded; the initial German attacks having taken their toll. Most of the men were quickly bandaged and sent back to their units. The more seriously hit lay on stretchers for the doctors to treat. Donnelly hated the place. The sight of so much blood and the heavy smell of disinfectant nauseated him.

Now Donnelly remembered the unopened envelope in his field jacket pocket. V-Mail from his mother, but he hadn't had time to open it before Task Force Coleman prepared to cross the Rhine.

He read the letter. In his state of mind, it was a series of impressions, no more. His brother, David, had gotten involved with a most undesirable girl before he left for infantry basic training. His father was one of three candidates up for appointment to a higher court, and, almost as an afterthought, his mother had added that a girl Charles had dated, Muffy, had married a middle-aged stock-broker and was about to have a baby. Charles shook his head, too preoccupied with what was going on around him to truly absorb what he had just read.

Finally, a medic knelt down beside him, swabbed the gash on his forehead, put a bandage around Donnelly's head and handed him a container of sulfa pills.

"Good as new?" Charles asked the medic.

"Can't tell, Lieutenant. If we wasn't cut off here on the east bank of this here river, I'd send you back to an evacuation hospital sure as hell. But ain't nothing more I can do. I done cleaned out all that dirt and disinfected and bandaged you up good. Now I got to send you back into the line."

✪

Donnelly had left the aid station before Buddy Marks showed up to check on him. So Buddy started back alone, heading up the gradual slope from the river. The aid station had been set up only a quarter of a mile away from the command post, well behind the fighting. Even so, Marks managed to get lost several times on his way back. He was taking his time, pausing to pick the new spring crocuses that peeked, purple and deep yellow, out of the black earth. He must have taken a wrong crossing at the last fork in the path, for he found himself in a quiet glade where a weathered old barn stood sentinel. Buddy stopped and listened. He couldn't hear the moans of the wounded anymore.

Three 88 shells screamed in and exploded in the field next to him. The sound of small arms and machine gun fire grew more insistent. Buddy scampered quickly back toward what he thought was the farmhouse and the colonel, but nothing looked right. He knew he was lost. Damn, he thought, Colonel Coleman will be waiting for me. How'd I get here? He stumbled through the woods, his large frame breaking branches as he went when, suddenly, he heard another sound, crystal clear. Somewhere close by, a woman screamed.

✪

Several minutes before, Colonel Coleman scrambled down the sharp embankment beyond the farmhouse and headed for a small rise in the woods that he had spotted from his command post. He had to get a better view of the developing battle. A vital radio link had just been broken, and they had no more communication with St. John or Turner. Had the Germans penetrated his right flank?

As he entered the woods, Coleman failed to see a somewhat dazed Charles Donnelly coming the other way, farther down the tree line, in search of the command post. Charles stood trying to get his bearings. He was startled to hear the roar of a diesel generator. His surprise turned to sheer terror when he realized what had happened. Some inexperienced, rear-echelon bastard had found the farmhouse generator and turned it on. The noise was sure to attract the attention of every German heavy gun in the vicinity. It was suicide.

Charles dove to earth as the first German shell screamed in. He was close enough to the C.P. to feel the shrieking, exploding cannon shells shake the ground beneath him. Trees uprooted, branches fell on his back. He put his hands over his head for protection and tried to wiggle his body deeper into the dirt, as something stung the top of his hand.

Just as suddenly as it had begun, the shelling stopped. Silence. Charles raised his head to look around, then slowly rose to his knees. The top of his hand bled from a small gash. He pulled open his first-aid pouch. Walking slowly in the direction from which he'd heard the now silent generator, he broke open the bandage container and wrapped up his hand.

When Charles finally made it to the top of the hill, he saw that the first few German shells had landed directly on the farmhouse and obliterated it. G.I.'s lay in all directions, some contorted in quiet death, others writhing in agony. Medics sprinted to the fallen soldiers. Clerks from the headquarters staff fumbled with bandages and morphine syrettes, attempting to be brave and useful. Several simply fainted on the spot. Donnelly sat on a knocked-down tree. He couldn't be much help with only one good hand. Exhausted and relieved to sit down, he figured that the Germans had long-range artillery back there somewhere, but they were short of shells. Otherwise, they'd have blown Task Force Coleman to pieces by now. Sliding gently off the log onto the ground, Donnelly passed out.

When he awoke, he didn't know how much time had passed. He stood up and surveyed the damage. Much of the mess had been cleaned up. The dead and wounded had been removed. The unhurt and walking wounded were getting organized, having converted several of the shell holes into bunkers by digging into the earth with shovels, helmets—anything they could find. Radio line-crews were back stringing wire.

Colonel Coleman had returned and stood on the far side of the rise, his face still registering shock and disbelief that such a stupid error could have occurred. Ramon Gonzalez-Rivera stood beside him, his hands full of communications wires.

Donnelly's hand had stopped bleeding, he noticed vaguely, though blood had soaked the rough bandage. Donnelly overheard Ramon reporting to Coleman, "I had just gotten the lines fixed when the place went up, Colonel. Now we'll have to start all over again. We were damned lucky most of the equipment was still at the river; otherwise, we'd be completely without radio communications."

Coleman looked out at the smoke on the horizon, and spoke with uncharacteristic detachment. "Take care of it, Major."

A hundred yards away, Coleman's men were still digging a temporary shelter to serve as a new command post. Coleman was betting that, having destroyed the farmhouse, the Germans would believe that the American headquarters would have to move elsewhere, and they would not waste any more of their precious shells up here. In any case, he had to have this high ground, even if it meant sleeping in a foxhole tonight.

Next to him, Gonzalez-Rivera scanned the distant hills. The major still felt exuberant at having survived his first taste of combat. Now he knew he could face death without flinching. "Looks like the Germans are pushing us a lot harder now," he said.

Coleman nodded and put a pair of field glasses to his eyes. "They haven't broken our lines. And the Baker Company platoon must have plugged the hole Sauter left or the Krauts would be into us good by now. My bet is they're understrength and badly led. They seem to have wasted the only armor they had when they let Donnelly bushwhack them. They're short of artillery and their infantry isn't very enthusiastic. They're just holding us until they can get some real muscle down here. I'll bet it's on the way right now. They'll plan to hit us tomorrow morning."

"They have us outnumbered and outgunned, sir," Gonzalez-Rivera said.

"You're new around here. My men will chew up those Krauts and eat them for breakfast. Just wait and see."

3

———

Colonel Lawrence Lightfoot Coleman stood near the bombed-out farmhouse that had served as his command post on the east bank of the Rhine, continuing to survey the damage from the generator catastrophe. His face showed strain as his officers reported the damage from the morning's fighting. The din of battle continued in the distance.

He still worried about his nephew, Lou Ames. Before he left for war, his older sister had admonished him, "I want you to make sure my boy comes back from this wretched war in once piece, Larry. I'm holding you responsible." A tall order, Coleman thought grimly. But it was an order he passed on to his subordinates.

Several officers approached the colonel with news of their battalions. To those who might know, the colonel asked, "Where the hell is Ames? I sent him to check our right flank an hour ago and haven't seen him since." Nor, it seemed, had anyone else.

Nearby, Lieutenant Charles Donnelly, fully awake, sat on a fallen log with a clean bandage on his forehead and a bloody one on his hand. Around him war had taken its toll. He turned his attention to Coleman and thought, Poor bastard—a whole platoon wiped out in an instant, his command post smashed to pieces, communications wires out. Task Force Coleman is coming apart at the seams. A disaster...

As if hearing the words, the colonel looked up and noticed Donnelly for the first time. "Charles," he said brusquely.

"Sir," said Donnelly, rising to his feet.

"Glad to see you back."

"Thank you, sir. You told me to report to you after the medics finished with me."

A winded Lieutenant John St. John trotted up, distracting Coleman. St. John was in a hurry and upset, which was rare.

"I have some bad news, sir," he said, his voice nearly cracking with emotion. "Sauter's platoon was wiped out in the minefield, as we figured. A Jerry company showed up, and I fought them for what seemed hours and was a goner, until Turner arrived and took control."

Coleman nodded. "Have you seen my nephew?" The colonel's voice sounded anxious.

"Yes, sir. At the minefield. He attracted the Jerries but didn't stay for the fun; said he was on his way back to report to you." There was a note of bitterness in John's voice.

"Damn, then he should be back by now," Coleman said.

Buddy Marks had returned and now leaned panting against a leafless tree. Everybody had been shaken by the shelling of the command post, but most had now recovered and were stringing wire or digging holes in an effort to put the task force headquarters back in functioning condition.

Catching sight of Buddy, the colonel called, "Hey, Marks! What are you doing hanging around over there?"

Marks took a large gulp of air, then walked over to Coleman. "I—I've got some terrible news, sir," he stammered.

Immediately, Coleman seemed apprehensive. "Is it about Lou?" Marks simply nodded.

"He's been hit?"

Buddy nodded.

"Bad?" Coleman's voice was anxious but controlled.

"He's killed, sir," blurted Marks. "Killed by one of our own men."

This simple statement left the other officers speechless. Coleman stared at Buddy in disbelief, the color draining from his face. He let out a deep breath. Gradually, he regained control. "You have to be mistaken. It was the mines, wasn't it? I'm sure it must've been the mines."

"No, sir," Marks said, his voice shaking. "He wasn't killed in the minefield."

Coleman stared at him. "He was checking Sauter's sector..."

"I heard screams, sir. I found him in a barn, murdered."

"Bloody Krauts." said Major Gonzalez-Rivera, who had just returned after sending his men out to lay wire. "Damned bloody Krauts!" He sounded as if he were trying to imitate John Wayne.

"They must still be in the area," added Donnelly.

Coleman shook his head. "That's not possible. We know there are no Germans inside our lines."

"May I speak to you alone, sir?" Buddy asked quietly.

"I'm sure that's not necessary, Marks. These officers can stay."

Buddy looked uncertainly towards St. John, Donnelly and Gonzalez-Rivera and seemed reluctant to speak in front of them.

"It's okay, Buddy."

Marks cleared his throat nervously. "Ames was still alive when I got to the barn. He said—he said he'd just been shot by an enlisted man. A bullet through the chest. I ran outside and saw a sergeant running into the woods, but I couldn't see his face. When I got back to the barn, Ames was dead."

Coleman stood for a moment, not seeming to understand. Finally, he turned to his officers. "Donnelly, the enemy doesn't have any tanks left. I'd like you and St. John to go to the barn with Lieutenant Marks and bring my nephew's body back. I hate to send three officers on a job like this, but Lou was my own flesh and blood, and I don't want to send anybody I don't know and trust. So get going."

Donnelly nodded solemnly. St. John shrugged with indifference. Charles had never known Ames except to say hello to, but, with the exception of the colonel, there was clearly not a lot of genuine grief in the group.

"I think it would be best if we kept this quiet until we can find out more about it," Coleman added.

"S—sir," Marks stammered. "There was a girl in the barn."

"What?" St. John shouted. "What do you mean?" He looked shocked.

"A German girl I think, sir. She'd been attacked…, well, raped, sir. Her clothes were torn and her throat was slit. I guess Ames was trying to save her and got himself killed."

Coleman turned his back to his officers. "Brave, stupid boy," he said. He raised his hand to his face to wipe away a tear.

As Donnelly, Marks and St. John rushed through the woods toward the body of Ames and the dead German girl, they could hear gunfire, both near and far, as battles continued unabated. Smoke drifted everywhere. It stung Charles's nostrils and eyes. He wondered if they'd be able to hold. He wondered whether or not he'd be dead by nightfall. After they entered the glade, though, things turned almost tranquil. He could hear the rustle of wind in the grass as they approached the old barn.

The barn doors creaked loudly as St. John threw them open. Ames's body lay just inside. He seemed oddly peaceful—his uniform was only slightly battle-stained, his .45 pistol still in its holster, and his head resting on the barn floor as if asleep. But the small red stain near his heart and the look of surprise on his face told the real story.

St. John hurried past Marks and knelt next to the body of the girl. He seemed to be in shock, as though all the deaths suffered in the war had never affected him until now. Donnelly and Marks came in quietly behind him and walked to the back of the barn.

St. John stared at the girl resting on a pile of strewn hay.

"Oh, God," he moaned, kneeling over the slain body. Her throat had been slit from ear to ear, and her once beautiful face was surrounded by a halo of blood that had stained the straw beneath her. Her brown gingham dress had been torn off, a small milk jug overturned next to her.

St. John looked appalled. A dead soldier was one thing. A horribly murdered civilian girl is something else. "What kind of monster could have done this?" he mumbled, more to himself than to anybody else. He turned to Marks. "Did Ames tell you anything else? Anything at all?"

Buddy shook his head. "He might have tried, but I never got close enough to hear him. I only poked my head in the door, then ran off looking for his killer. Maybe, if I hadn't done that, I could have saved him. I guess I wasn't thinking," he said mournfully.

"You couldn't have done anything for him," St. John muttered. "He was dead."

"Strange way to go," said Donnelly as he watched St. John and Marks gently lift Ames's body onto the canvas stretcher they'd brought along for the purpose. "He was killed trying to save a Kraut's life. Ironic."

St. John peered back at the girl. "Charles, please, cover her up. She looks so cold lying there, poor thing." As if to hide the tears in his voice, St. John tossed Donnelly the blanket that came with the stretcher.

"What should we do with the body?" asked Donnelly. He had purposely kept his eyes averted so as not to look at her even as he draped the blanket over her.

"We"ll come back for her…, or send somebody. Criminal Investigation Division will want to have a look. Whoever did this will get the rope just as sure as there's a hell. Rape's a hanging offense. Add on murder—"

"Maybe one of us should wait here with her," suggested Donnelly.

St. John nodded. "Yes, I'll wait. You two take him." There wasn't a trace of his usual nonchalance. "How could this happen?" he said finally, clearly moved and horrified by the sight of the raped girl lying there, so innocent and so ravaged.

"Donnelly!" Colonel Coleman called out from the makeshift door of his new command post. The afternoon sun hung low, and Charles had returned from the grisly task. The bodies of Ames and the girl had been delivered to the aid station.

Charles hurried over to Coleman to make his report. "Sir, we turned your nephew over to the aid station. Sergeant Price asked if there were any special orders."

Coleman nodded absently. "I'll go down if I can. It looks like the task force is going to make it," he said, his eyes fixed, as ever, on the distant battlefields. "We've been under attack all day, but the German units haven't been strong enough to penetrate our positions."

"Heavy casualties?" Donnelly asked.

"Pretty bad," Coleman confirmed. "Still, if the enemy had more armor, or if they'd held back their Tigers until they knew which were the weaker spots in our line, they might have finished us off. We got lucky. Now, it's up to General Patton."

Charles stood silently, digesting what had been left unsaid. If Patton didn't get the Fifth Infantry Division across tonight and draw off the German attack, the task force would most certainly be wiped out. Charles prayed that General Patton would succeed, as he always did. But it would be a long night of waiting for events to happen. A long night of not knowing.

The two men stood for a moment, watching the sun sink over the Rhine.

"Thank you for taking care of that business this afternoon," Coleman said finally. Donnelly could hear the traces of weariness and sorrow in his voice. "Please go tell the sergeant that I'll be down a bit later."

Coleman watched Donnelly head down the hill into the deepening dusk.

"Sir?" It was Gonzalez-Rivera approaching from behind.

"How do things look, Ramon? Any news?"

"I think we ought to try to get back across the river tonight, sir. If we wait until tomorrow, they might hit us with everything they've got, and we won't have a chance."

"No faith, Ramon?"

"Sure, Colonel, I have plenty of faith. But we've done our job. We've accomplished what we came to do. So, now, why don't we just get the hell out of here?"

Coleman shook his head. "Our orders are to stay here until the Fifth Division crosses, so we'll stay here until the Fifth crosses. Understand?"

"Yes, sir." The major cleared his throat. "Again, I can't tell you how sorry I am about your nephew, sir."

"Thank you, Ramon. So am I. He was all his mother had. I don't know how to break the news to her."

"We'll find the man who did this, sir."

"Yes, I hope so. But at what price to the regiment?" Coleman asked, clearly worried. "Once C.I.D. gets their hands on this, every one of my men will be under suspicion."

"Perhaps we could keep C.I.D. out of the investigation for a while, sir," Gonzalez-Rivera said thoughtfully. "Do some of the groundwork ourselves—keep things on the inside until we have a few more facts. After all, we're cut off over here right now, anyway."

"I don't know..."

"Just for a few days, sir, until things have calmed down a bit. It won't hurt the men any to think Lou was killed by the Jerries."

"Perhaps you're right, Ramon. Still, C.I.D. will have my ass if they find out we delayed an investigation."

"We aren't delaying it, Colonel. We're just doing their work for them," Gonzalez-Rivera insisted.

"I'll think over what you've said," Coleman said. Dismissing his officer, the colonel went back to his radios. He had to keep in close contact with his depleted infantry units so that he could move his already exhausted reserve platoons where they were most needed.

While his crew cleaned the gun, Donnelly plopped next to a fallen tree to write home. There was still enough light, but there wouldn't be if he waited much longer. He kept in touch with his family through letters to his mother. He now had time to digest her last letter and reply to it. He asked what was so "impossible" about his brother David's girlfriend, what was the name of the stockbroker Muffy had married, whether his father got the judicial appointment; then he realized he was merely answering her letter and contributing nothing about what he was doing. So, he lied. He told his mother he was in a safe area, working behind a desk, that an infantry antitank company just counted the tanks the armored divisions had knocked out, and a lot of other misinformation to keep her from worrying about him. It never occurred to him that the Army might advise her he'd been wounded in action. He stuck his pencil in his mouth and sucked on it a minute. What else could he tell her? Finally, he decided to fill her in on how beautiful the scenery was and how the lovely rivers and fields of flowers delighted him. He implored her to write and keep him advised of what was going on in Chicago. As a postscript, he told her he hadn't met any beautiful girls yet, and, besides, it was against the rules to even talk to any German except on official business. Content, he sealed the letter, not knowing when he'd get a chance to send it.

Charles and his three men were fast asleep beside their gun, when he felt someone kicking him gently. Charles pointed his .45 pistol into the night and was startled to see Colonel Coleman. He scrambled to his feet.

"Sir?" he whispered.

Silently, Coleman beckoned Donnelly to follow him. They walked a short distance away from the gun and sat down under a fir tree whose overhanging boughs touched the cold ground, hiding them from the other men. Charles watched Coleman's haggard face, though it was barely visible in the darkness.

"I don't want to wake the men," the colonel whispered finally. "They had a rough day and need to sleep. You posted guards?"

"No, sir. First Battalion said we could sleep within their lines."

"Donnelly, I don't have much time, so I'll get right to the point. I want you to investigate my nephew's murder—talk to some of the men quietly, see if you can find out anything."

"Me, sir?" Charles asked in surprise.

"You were studying to be a criminal lawyer, weren't you? You told me once that you were."

"Yes, sir, but that's different. The C.I.D. should handle this. The Army's full of officers trained for this type of work. I'm an infantryman."

"It'll take time for C.I.D. to get somebody up here. I need an officer to follow the trail immediately, before it gets cold. We move out tomorrow morning, if we're lucky. You'll stay behind after we've gone and examine the barn—see if the killer left any clues, anything at all that might help us narrow this down. Then, I'd like you to talk to Marks. Find out exactly what happened. Pin him down. He can be a bit vague."

"Sir, I really think—"

Coleman waved his hand, silencing Donnelly. "Listen to me very carefully, Charles," he said, leaning forward to give weight to his words. "Until we find the man who did this, we'll be carrying him with us like a virus. This soldier has raped and murdered. What's to stop him from killing again? We must act quickly."

"Yes, sir."

Charles knew he wouldn't be able to sleep after Coleman's assignment.

Later that evening, he made his way to the aid station. He had no difficulty finding the sergeant in charge, a man named Price. He motioned to the sergeant and said, "Price, come with me." Together the two men walked to the area where the dead were laid out in rows, covered with blankets, ponchos, or army raincoats.

"Where is the body of Lieutenant Ames?" asked Donnelly.

"Over there with the other officers. I'll take you." As they walked, the sergeant added, "They brought in a girl, too, sir. We've got her wrapped in a blanket inside that shed over there. Is that all right, sir? The Graves Registration people will pick up the dead as soon as they can get to us. When they come, we can turn her over to them then."

Donnelly shuddered.

When the sergeant removed the blanket that covered Ames, Charles drew in a breath. He'd seen bodies before, but not laid out like this, stark and stiff.

"I have his personal effects, if you want to take them to the colonel, sir. They haven't been sorted out or anything, just what we took from his pockets, stuff that was on him."

"No, thank you. Do you know if the colonel wants them?"

Price thought for a minute. "No, sir. I think he's too cut up about his nephew getting killed to want to take the stuff. He'll probably want it sent to the lieutenant's mother or something.

"I have the lieutenant's web belt and .45 pistol, too."

"Why the pistol?" asked Donnelly. "It's government issue."

"Didn't know what else to do with it, sir. Our supply and ordinance people got knocked off in the shelling."

"Why don't you hang on to the lieutenant's things until we get the matter sorted out, Price? Including the pistol. They're probably safer here with you than anywhere else."

"I'll do that, sir."

"And the girl's body. Don't include her with the dead German soldiers. Hold her for C.I.D."

"Yes, sir."

In the early sunrise, Charles stood, once again, outside the barn. The surrounding wooded hills and open fields that had been a battleground hours ago lay quiet now that Task Force Coleman had left to link up with the Fourth Armored Division.

Though Charles had been in this same spot yesterday, today he tried to inspect the barn with the eyes of a detective. It was weather-beaten, not large by American standards, with wide spaces between the wooden planking. Charles cautiously peered through one of the gaps in the slats. Had Ames stood here for a moment and seen the rape before going in to save the girl? Charles went to the large door and opened it. It creaked loudly. Ames could not have gotten in without being heard. Had this door been Ames's death warrant, alerting the killer before Ames got a chance to draw his own gun? He had seen it still in its holster.

Inside, Charles was sure he would still feel death in the fetid air, but he felt only a mild chill. He walked gingerly, not wishing to disturb anything that might be considered evidence to his untrained mind, although he knew that any useful clues would probably have been trampled under foot when they had come yesterday to collect the bodies. As his eyes became accustomed to the semi-darkness of the barn, he saw the recess where the girl must have been eating her breakfast that morning when the fighting broke out. A crust of black bread and a small bottle of milk still lay in the shadows. Had she stolen away to meet a lover in the barn? Had her father sent her out to retrieve something? When the gunfire started, she'd have been trapped inside, undoubtedly terrified. All she could have done was wait for the fighting to stop. But it turned out differently. He'd like to see whoever had done this hanged. How strange, Donnelly thought, as he knelt down beside the blood-stained piles of hay, that he felt such compassion for a German girl—an enemy.

Using a long stick, Charles sifted through the scattered straw, hoping to find a shell from the rifle that had shot Ames—the killer would have been here at the back of the barn with the girl when Ames stumbled in. But his careful search of the ground revealed nothing.

Charles walked to the front of the barn, scanning the floor for any clue. His eyes moved up the wall, looking for a glint of metal. Any stray bullets the rapist might have shot would have lodged here. But there was nothing. Discouraged, he leaned back against the barn wall.

"Dammit!" A long nail jutting out of the unfinished wood had pierced him in the back. As his turned to see what he had leaned on, he noticed a small piece of cloth hanging from a similar nail on the next plank. It was a torn strip of olive drab fabric. Army issue, without a doubt, the scrap of a field jacket. Charles took off his own jacket to see if it was torn, but there was no rip in it of any kind. Charles took the torn cloth off the nail. He stood there a moment, looking around the barn. Then, deciding that there was nothing else here that would be of any help, he left, thoughtfully fingering the piece of material in his pocket. Perhaps Ames had torn his uniform. He would have to examine the corpse to find out. But if it wasn't from Lou's field jacket, then perhaps this piece of cloth had come from the killer's. It was a small thing, an outside chance, yet for now it was all he had.

4

⬥

Charles left the barn and went down to the aid station to examine Ames's corpse again, worrying that he would have to face Coleman's wrath with nothing but a scrap of cloth to show for his investigation. In order to prepare the wounded for transport, the aid station had remained behind when the infantry moved out.

Immediately Charles found Price and asked, "May I see Ames's body again?"

"Yes, sir," said Price. "You're just in time. That Graves Registration squad you see there is preparing to remove the dead."

Charles turned Ames onto his stomach and examined the back of his field jacket. No tear. He then looked at Ames and tried to be detached, despite detesting touching dead bodies. Quickly, he examined the rest of the field jacket and found not so much as a loose thread. Ames's hands were both clenched into fists. He might have grabbed something off of his murderer, thought Charles. He tried in vain to unclench the cold, stiff hands. "Sergeant Price," he called. "Please help me pry these hands open." Together they managed it. One hand was empty. The other held a pouch intended to carry two .45 clips for a pistol. Donnelly kept it, then nodded to Sergeant Price and the Graves Registration squad leader that he'd finished his examination.

Why, thought Donnelly, would Lou Ames be clutching a .45 pouch? He opened it. Only one clip inside. Turning it over, Charles saw immediately that the hooks on the back had been torn open, and a tiny metal eyelet ring dangled from one side, as if the pouch had been torn from a web belt with some force, as if Ames had grabbed hold of his killer's waist and held onto the pouch before falling to the ground. Donnelly's excitement mounted.

"Now, may I see the girl?" he asked, wondering why he hadn't thought of that before. When he had gone to the barn that day, he had purposely avoided looking at her. The idea had only just come to him as he spoke to Price and the Graves Registration sergeant, who had just joined them.

The body lay apart from the German dead. An army blanket encased her from head to foot like an Egyptian mummy. The idea of uncovering her was distasteful to Donnelly, yet he knew it had to be done. Charles felt embarrassed examining a naked woman, especially one he knew had been so mutilated. With clammy, shaking hands, his head woozy, and his stomach churning, he knelt to unwrap the body. He touched his finger to the edge of the blanket, then recoiled in automatic revulsion. He wanted to just yank it off like a bandage but knew that wouldn't be right. He nervously glanced around. He was alone with the girl's body. That was good. No prying eyes. Slowly, Donnelly carefully pulled back the blanket from the top of her head. The girl's hair was the color of honey. It was long and graceful. Continuing to remove the blanket, he discovered a lovely alabaster-like face, perfectly proportioned. Her lips were now blue, her brown eyes still open. Donnelly, in an automatic reaction, closed them. When he pulled the blanket back further, he saw the scarlet trench gouged in the girl's throat. He had time to turn his head just before he threw up his breakfast. Still heaving, he returned to his gruesome task. The girl's petite body was as near perfect as it could be, but her otherwise flawless breasts showed scratches. So did the rest of her torso. Glancing back at her perfect face, he carefully turned it to the other side. There it showed bruises. There was no doubt in Donnelly's mind that the girl had been brutally raped. She reminded him of a gorgeous flower that had been crushed by a cruel boot. He wished desperately that she could tell him who had done this to her.

Trembling, he took one of her hands. Yes, the nails were broken and ragged. Yes, she'd fought hard. He took the other. The same, except for a ring on the little finger. Donnelly lifted her hand and studied the ring closely. It was a simple, inexpensive silver band with two roses entwined on the front. Lovely and feminine and, to Charles, exquisite in its simplicity. He knew he'd remember it long after the unpleasantness of murder.

✪

"Something wrong, boss?"

Charles turned to see his driver standing beside his Jeep. None of the regiment's drivers had made the crossing, not even Coleman's. The only vehicle to go over was the Jeep towing the anti-tank gun, which Charles drove himself.

"Nothing you can help me with, Montana," Charles said grimly. Montana was cleanly dressed without any trace of battle to stain his uniform. Tall, lanky with laughing eyes and a deeply lined face, Montana looked like a typical cowboy. He was good-natured, except when somebody called him by his real name, which was Mortimore Hackett, and he had been Donnelly's driver ever since Charles had come into the outfit, when they had established an easy rapport. Donnelly liked him and counted on him. Moreover, Montana, unlike the enlisted men who crossed with the task force, was not under suspicion of murder.

As the Jeep made its way eastward to catch up with the regiment, Charles stared at the debris that the avenging American army had left in its wake. The road was rutted and shell-pocked. Burned-out, shrapnel-shattered vehicles lined its edges. Knocked-out vehicles had been shoved off onto the shoulders to make a path for the traffic on its way up to the line: trucks hauling artillery pieces or ammunition and rations, halftracks, antitank guns, Jeeps, and occasional convoys bringing up infantry replacements. Nobody was observing road discipline. A couple of German fighter planes could have wiped out the whole lot of them. And Montana and Donnelly rode smack in the middle of it all.

Seeing the mayhem around him reminded Donnelly of how fortunate he was to be in a good outfit with a regimental commander like Larry Coleman. Though he could be tough—and certainly Charles wanted no part of confronting him today—Coleman had the magic that turned a mere mass of troops into a formidable weapon. Even before the Rhine crossing, he'd proved himself many times over. But the Rhine crossing was the crowning accomplishment that would probably earn Coleman his promotion to general.

It was dusk when they finally arrived at the small German town selected to be their new headquarters. The houses were brightly painted with blue or green window shutters and flower boxes in front. Charles noted that the regiment had commandeered them, hanging tarpaulins and blankets over the windows, and he imagined they'd lit candles inside. Far away in the night, the growling of artillery sounded like distant thunder.

Charles jumped out of the Jeep in front of the headquarters building, which normally served as the town hall, just as several truckloads of replacements pulled out for the battalions. "See you later, Montana. Make sure you put the Jeep in a safe place if you don't take it back to the motor pool." He winked. Montana liked to roam. Waving goodbye, Donnelly entered the building and bumped directly into Marks.

"Hey, Buddy. Where's the colonel?"

"He went over to Baker Company to talk to Captain Turner. The colonel's been asking for you."

"Welcome home, Charles." Donnelly turned, pleased to see St. John ambling toward him. "Good lord," continued John, "you look like something out of an old war movie."

Charles grinned sheepishly.

"You really ought to cover up that obscene bandage with your new helmet."

"Go to hell. I received my wounds honorably." Charles grinned. "Besides, it makes me look like a real hero. We chicken-hearted weaklings need all the help we can get."

Johnny laughed. "Well, you may as well show it off while you can. Chances are you won't be getting hit much any more. You're not going back to Antitank Company."

"Why?"

"You're staying right here. Didn't Buddy tell you?"

"I didn't have time," said Marks.

"Buddy's getting a promotion. He'll be moving on to bigger and better pastures. And since Lou Ames checked out, Coleman needs a new right-hand man. Seems it's going to be you. You look surprised," said John.

"I thought..." Charles stopped. The others had no idea that Coleman had assigned him to investigate Ames's murder. "It's just that I never thought of myself as a rear-echelon type," he said quickly, then turned to Marks. "Has the colonel found out anything about Ames?"

"Nothing. He questioned a few of the men, but they were all accounted for on the battlefield. He sent a report to C.I.D. yesterday. So I guess it's in their hands now."

St. John shook his head. "The C.I.D. won't do a thing. We all know that. But then, how can they? A thousand guys could have done it. No one saw anything. And even if they did, they'd never say so."

"What do you mean?" Charles asked.

"Oh, you know how the men are," St. John said off-handedly. "They close ranks and protect each other, just as we would."

Charles nodded. "What about the girl?" he asked. "Has her family been contacted?"

St. John shifted his feet and spoke with a raspy voice. "Don't worry about that. I'm sure it will be taken care of."

Moments later, Donnelly heard the colonel's voice coming down the hallway. Captain Paul Turner accompanied him, swearing up a storm. Turner's years as an enlisted man in the regular army had given him a distinctive vocabulary.

"This is bullshit, Colonel. You hear? I'll vouch for every one of my men. If you start questioning them I'll have a goddam war on my hands!"

"That's enough, Turner."

Donnelly moved toward them and was about to salute, when Turner said, "Son of a bitch, if it ain't the Tiger Killer." He was smiling, but Donnelly thought he could detect a faint challenge in his voice.

"Lieutenant," Coleman said to Donnelly, "starting immediately, you're going to help me run my headquarters. So, go get whatever gear you have over at Antitank and come move in."

Turner laughed and said, "So you're getting out of Antitank, huh, Charlie? Gonna be a rear-echelon bastard with all the rest of them cock—"

Coleman cut in, "Watch it, Captain, or you'll be joining headquarters, too—as a private."

"You know I belong with the men at the front, sir," said Turner. "I'm strictly a combat man. I'd be like tits on a boar hog in any headquarters."

"You'll do as I say, no matter what I say, and that's the end of it. Now, Captain Turner, get moving!"

Turner left, scowling.

"You too, Charles." Coleman's voice was now friendly, as usual.

"I don't know where Antitank is now, sir."

"I'll take you over," said St. John and the colonel nodded his agreement. Donnelly had already surmised that Coleman was pulling him out of Antitank so he could concentrate on the investigation of the murder.

Outside, as Donnelly watched Turner screeching away in his Jeep, he was glad that St. John, not Turner, was driving him over to his old company's billets. He knew Turner was a good officer, but Turner had an ill-concealed hostility towards him and the other officers. The only exception was Buddy Marks, who Turner seemed to like and whom he watched over like a son.

Turner did not trust other men easily. Donnelly had sensed that from the first time they met. And, while Donnelly's heroism against the Tigers had not escaped Turner's notice, apparently he was still reserving judgment.

St. John was a different bird, Donnelly thought, as he climbed into the front seat next to him. St. John's studied nonchalance amused Charles, especially his posturing as a bored aristocrat on the way to the guillotine. Though he behaved like an Eastern preppie, he once told Charles that he had been an actor before the war. His movie star good looks would probably have made his career a success. But when the war broke out, despite his lack of formal education, John's high I.Q. got him into Officers Candidate School, where he discovered a skill and penchant for war, a discipline that made him a fine soldier. Twice decorated, St. John was already a captain. While Charles hated everything about the war, the danger and excitement were a tonic to St. John. He was always out in front, always seemed cool under fire. Donnelly wondered how they had ever become such close friends.

Charles sat next to St. John as they sped down a tiny cobbled street. "You know, Johnny, I never got a chance to ask you: How in hell did you manage to hold off all those Jerries until Turner showed up?"

Johnny shrugged easily. "Oh, Charles, it was nothing. I just dodged a few bullets and got off a few good shots. It was all very tedious."

Charles smiled. "You were out there all alone with forty Krauts bearing down on you and you weren't scared at all?"

"Not for a second."

"So, how'd you do it?"

"I was in a long ditch," John replied. "About shoulder deep. I'd run down to one end, pop up and let loose with my Tommy gun at whatever I saw move, then duck down and run in the opposite direction and do the same thing. I wanted them to think they were up against a battalion instead of just one lousy guy. Of course, if they'd known it was me, Juggernaut Johnny, they'd have retreated in a hurry."

Charles interrupted. "Don't you mean Jackass Johnny?"

"I admit, I was mildly concerned when they started throwing mortar rounds into my ditch. Then, every time I got up to shoot at the bastards, there were more of them, moving closer and closer. I'm quite sure I could have handled it on my own, but Paul Turner showed up to lend a hand."

"You mean, to save your life."

"Charles, don't be so dramatic."

St. John took a sharp left onto an unpaved road that led to a large house. The Jeep stopped in front of the house and Charles hopped out. "Won't be a minute."

Charles picked up his meager possessions at the Antitank Company billet, stopping to tell Cousins, Novak, and Russo that they were all getting medals for their bravery on the gun and to please advise the captain, who was out, that Donnelly was being transferred to headquarters. Then he left to join St. John in the Jeep.

After the drive back to headquarters, St. John invited Donnelly up to his room for a drink.

"Thanks. I could use one."

Inside St. John's ground floor room, John checked that the blankets that covered his two windows were tight and secure. Then he took a candle from his field jacket pocket, lit it and stuck it in the neck of a bottle. The room was bare, except for a small table, two chairs and Johnny's bedroll stored in the corner of the room. The walls had not been painted for a long time.

Johnny stuck his hand inside his bedroll and dug around. "Voilà!" he announced, pulling out a silver flask. "It was my father's. Poor old lush drank himself to death. I thought this was a fitting memento." Johnny took a swig and handed it to Charles. "It's not cognac, but it'll do in a pinch."

"Here's to love," said Charles, for no reason he could think of. He handed the flask back to St. John.

Johnny raised it. "Why not?" he said, and drank deeply. "Ever been in love, Charles?"

Donnelly shook his head slowly. "Don't think so. You?"

St. John passed the flask back. He didn't answer as he watched Charles take a short gulp. Then, he nodded. "Yes, I'd say so."

"Girl from New York, I suppose?"

John was silent for a moment. "Actually," he said, "I met her over here."

"English, then?"

John smiled. "Bug off, Charles! You sound like my late mother."

Whatever was in the flask, Charles found himself reeling with exhaustion after his few sips. "I think it's bedtime for this soldier," he said abruptly. "See you tomorrow."

"I'm off early to do a bit of recon… visit the line companies."

"Have a glorious day, Johnny."

"Like a walk in the park."

Charles strolled as steadily as he could down the hall to his own first floor room. There he was dismayed to find a message on his table instructing him to report to Colonel Coleman in his bedroom upstairs.

Charles tapped lightly at the colonel's second story door.

"Come in," growled Coleman's familiar voice.

The room looked like the former bürgermeister's office with heavy, dark brown, Teutonic furniture. There were some conspicuous squares of unfaded paint on the walls where portraits of Hitler, Goering, and Goebbels had undoubtedly hung.

The colonel, still dressed, sat in a chair reading reports by a kerosene lamp. He looked up as Donnelly came in. "Ah, Charles. I've been waiting for you."

"Sorry, sir. I stopped by St. John's room on my way back."

"I hope he didn't force you to drink that rotgut he carries around," Coleman laughed. "Sit down, Charles, sit down." Without preamble he said, "I've recommended you for the Congressional Medal of Honor. For knocking out three Tiger tanks and stopping the Panzer attack that day at the Rhine."

"Thank you, sir," Charles said. "But I really don't think I deserve it."

"I happen to think you do. So, if you get it, please accept it gracefully. More than that, I wanted to be the one to tell you: You're promoted to first lieutenant." He held out his fist and opened it to reveal two silver bars, one for each of Donnelly's collars.

As Charles reached out and took the bars, Coleman's expression changed. "Now. I'd like to know how things are going with your investigation. Anything to report?"

"Sir, I stopped by the aid station to examine Ames's body."

"Tell me what you found out."

Charles shifted nervously. "I went to the barn early this morning, following your orders. I searched the place but the only thing I found was a strip of material. It's obviously off an American field jacket." Donnelly pulled the scrap from his pocket.

Coleman nodded grimly. "Can I take a look?"

"Of course, sir." Donnelly handed him the cloth.

"Well, then, let's take a look at all the field jackets in the whole damned regiment!" Coleman thundered.

"With all due respect, sir, once the men find out what we're doing, whoever owns the field jacket will destroy it or hide it or get rid of it somehow, and we'll get nowhere. So I suggest, sir, you allow me to investigate this matter privately, and perhaps, catch our man before he suspects anything."

Coleman took a cigar from his battered cigar box as he considered the request. "And Lou? Were there any clues there?"

"Well yes, sir. Ames was clutching a .45 pouch—one clip missing. I examined his field jacket, and there was no tear. The strip of cloth definitely didn't come from Lou's uniform and neither did the ammo pouch."

"So, you have made progress." The colonel sounded pleased. With a wooden match, Coleman lit his corona, then slowly blew a stream of grey smoke into the air. "When you left the aid station after getting hit yesterday, did you go anywhere near the barn where Buddy found Lou's body?"

"No, I don't think so," said Charles, thoughtfully. "At least, I don't remember any barn. But I was still pretty shaken up."

"I was wondering if you might have seen something in that vicinity. Johnny says he saw Lou at Sauter's sector before that."

It was strange that Johnny hadn't mentioned Lou to him just now, Charles thought. Aloud he said, "I understand from St. John that you alerted C.I.D."

"Yes. I decided I had to."

"I assume this means I'm off the case, sir."

"On the contrary, Charles. Why do you think I transferred you to headquarters? I want you to keep at it. Talk to the men quietly. Someone is bound to remember something. Criminal Investigations Division won't get anywhere. They rarely do." Coleman paused. "Really get cracking, Charles."

"Sir, I'll do my best."

"Your best is very good, Charles. I want Lou's killer found! Understood?" Coleman raised his voice uncharacteristically. "I'm sorry, Charles. But you must understand, I grew up idolizing my sister. Helen was ten years older than I was and after our parents died, Helen became my mother as well as my sister. She was all I had. And Lou was all she had—her husband died in a plane crash when Lou was nine. I'm afraid she spoiled him rotten, but he was her life, and she never could refuse him anything. I promised her I would protect Lou. I broke that promise. But I will find his killer, of that much I am certain."

Donnelly shifted awkwardly. The responsibility of all this lay on his inept shoulders, and he realized for the first time that

Coleman would never release him from the investigation until the murder was solved.

"Shall I go through Ames's things?" asked Charles.

"Hell, yes. You should have done that before now."

"Yes, sir."

5

Sun streamed through the cracks in the old pine shutters that covered Donnelly's window when he awoke the next morning. He looked at his watch, jumped out of bed and threw open the door. He should have been up hours ago. Outside, Jeeps and men moved through the tiny streets of the old German town. Most civilians had been moved to an abandoned factory on the far side of the village, but there were signs of normal life everywhere: laundry hung from lines between the low buildings; across the way in the upstairs window of a small stone house, Donnelly saw the glint of a gilded bird cage, and a spot of yellow, as a canary flitted about on its bar.

Donnelly pulled on his boots and went down the hall to find something to eat. A round of cheese and a some unbroken eggs, which he promptly fried on the wood burning stove made a good breakfast, much better than K rations, anyway. Charles ate quickly and went in search of Sergeant Price. After asking a few men, he found Price overseeing the unloading of a medical supply truck.

"Sergeant Price?" he called from behind the sergeant's back.

"Yes? What is it?" Price said impatiently, not bothering to look up from his inventory list.

"The colonel asked me to speak to you."

"Can't you see I'm busy?" Price's brusque tone changed at once as he turned and saw Donnelly. "Sorry, Lieutenant, I thought you was one of the boys. What can I do for you?"

"I'd like to take a look at Lieutenant Ames's personal effects.
I assume you still have them for safekeeping."

"No problem, sir. Come with me."

Price was a feisty fireplug of a man—short, stocky, and quick.
He reminded Donnelly of James Cagney.

Donnelly followed him. They turned left down a side street
that opened onto a playing field. A schoolhouse stood on the corner.

"This is where we've set up shop, for the moment." Price
opened the wide double doors of the school. Children's drawings still
lined the hallways. Tiny easels leaned against the wall in one corner,
and smocks, spattered with watercolors, hung on low metal hooks.
The corridor had the sour smell of cheese and sausages, not at all like
Charles remembered from his own childhood.

Price opened the door of a classroom, where a first-aid
supply room had been set up. He took a key out of the teacher's
desk drawer and unlocked a tall cupboard, pulled out a medium-
sized canvas bag and dumped it on the desk.

"It's all yours, sir. I'm gonna finish that unloading. It'll only
be a few minutes, then I'll be back here if you need me."

"Fine."

After Price left, Donnelly sat in the stillness of the room
holding the bag in his hands, as if the feel of it would reveal something to him. These were the last things that Ames had touched, or
that had touched Ames. Charles emptied the bag on a nearby
school desk and spread out the contents, hoping against hope that
one of the objects on the desktop might give him a clue to Ames's
killer. He wished that he had known Ames. But Charles had never
had any occasion to work with, or socialize with, the boy. Ames
stayed close to his uncle, and Charles was always out with his gun
crews. Maybe that was the reason Coleman put him in charge of
the investigation. He didn't know Ames. But then, it seemed that
nobody who knew him wanted to talk about him. Who were his
friends, Charles wondered. He'd have to find out from St. John or
Montana.

He picked up the web belt that Ames had been wearing when he was killed and examined it closely. There were no eyelets torn from Ames's belt. The belt was in good shape. He turned it over. The inside of the web belt was marked with Ames's name and serial number. The pistol was still in its russet leather holster; a first-aid packet and twin clip pouch were hooked to its eyelets. He took Ames's .45 out of its holster and released the clip. Full. He pulled back the receiver and a .45 caliber bullet flipped out. He opened the clip pouch. Also full. The poor son of a bitch had never even gotten a shot off.

On the table were Lou Ames's meager possessions—a stainless steel wristwatch, some change, a couple of condoms, a wallet with Lou's driver's license, a photograph and a few dollar bills he'd kept, a pencil, some bunched-up writing paper, a candle and some keys. From inside Lou Ames's wallet, the much-creased photograph showed a beautiful young woman sitting on a swing holding a small child in her lap, her head thrown back in laughter. A handsome man in pilot's gear stood behind her, his hand resting on her shoulder; a somber teenaged boy leaned against a fence in the background. Charles looked at the photo more closely. The boy on the fence was Colonel Coleman, he realized. The woman must be his sister, Helen.

Charles heard the door open behind him.

"Everything all right, sir?" Price deposited a box of syringes on the floor next to the desk.

"Under the circumstances, I suppose so." Charles sighed.

"Who's the dame?" Price pointed to the photo in Donnelly's hand.

"Colonel Coleman's sister." Charles smiled. "A long time ago."

"Nice. So what's this all about, anyway?"

"The usual Army business," Charles said evasively.

"Right," Price answered skeptically. "Funny business— between you and me, sir."

"Oh?"

"Rumor has it Ames was killed by one of us."

"Where did you hear that?" Charles asked quickly.

Price side-stepped the question. "Seems C.I.D. is coming up to investigate. If the Jerries got Ames then there's no need for C.I.D. to come sniffing around."

"So you think that Ames was accidentally killed by one of our own soldiers?" Donnelly probed.

Price shrugged. "Accidentally? I ain't never heard of C.I.D. checking up on guys killed by friendly fire, Lieutenant, if you get my meaning. And I certainly ain't never heard of a man shot straight through the heart at close range by mistake, sir." Price sat down on the edge of the desk.

"Who told you C.I.D. was coming in to investigate?"

Price shrugged. "Colonel Coleman, sir."

"How many of the men know about this?"

"Just me and Jimmy Smith—the medic who examined Lieutenant Ames."

"Listen Price, I suggest you keep your theories to yourself for now, or Coleman will have you for breakfast. And tell Smith the same."

"I ain't no fool, Lieutenant. If Coleman wants to wait for C.I.D., then we'll wait. And Smith don't say 'Boo!' without my permission."

"Where is this Smith?"

"He's around. Can't miss him—huge hook nose and a bunch of red hair. You want me to tell him you're looking for him?"

"That's okay. I'll find him myself."

"So what are you, sir? Like a private eye or something?" Price sounded honestly interested. His tone was friendly, but curious.

"Hardly," Charles laughed.

"So how come you want to know about Ames?"

That's a good question, Charles thought to himself. Aloud he said, "Coleman asked me to find out anything I can. Unofficially, of course."

"No problem, sir."

Twenty minutes later, Charles found Jimmy Smith checking the contents of an ambulance in front of the medical detachment's billets. As Price had said, he was impossible to miss.

"Smith? I'm Lieutenant Donnelly. I'd like a quick word."

"L—l—look, Lieutenant," Smith stuttered. "I don't know nothing, okay, sir?"

Price, it seemed, had already given him Donnelly's warning.

"It's all right, Smith. I just need to ask you a few things. Price said that Ames was shot at close range. Why did he say that?"

The medic looked at Donnelly as though the answer was obvious, even to an officer. "Powder burns."

"Of course." They had never looked closely at Ames when they had gone to fetch him, and Charles had been too upset to notice when he viewed the body.

"Did you find a bullet in the body?"

"Parts of it, sir. Them .45 slugs goes in and spreads out. Rips a guy's insides to pieces."

"But Ames was shot with a rifle."

"That wasn't no rifle wound, sir."

"How can you be so sure?"

"Hell, sir, I've seen enough bullet wounds to last me ten lifetimes. That was a .45's work or I'm Betty Grable."

As he walked back towards the town hall where the headquarters officers were billeted, Charles thought about the implications of what he had just learned. Was it possible that Buddy had misunderstood Ames? Everyone said the gentle giant was a bit slow-witted, but how could he make a mistake like that? He would have to find Buddy and question him right away.

He wished that St. John were here; he badly needed a friend to talk things over with. Unfortunately, John was out visiting the line companies, getting to know the rifle company officers and the artillery forward observers. He had to work with them all from time to time, and the high casualty rates kept them changing frequently.

St. John was the only one who knew about Charles's investigation. Charles had kept his promise to Coleman and said nothing. But Johnny didn't miss a thing, and had confronted Charles about it in the hallway last night just after Charles had left Coleman's room. Charles had been too tired to lie about his new role and, in truth, it was a relief to talk about it to someone he trusted. And besides that, St. John seemed as eager to solve the murder as Coleman.

Donnelly found Buddy in his room cleaning his boots with an old rag. Marks always managed to appear neat and orderly, despite trousers and a field jacket stained with grease spots. Now, sitting on the edge of what must have been a child's bed, he looked so big and awkward that Charles felt a wave of compassion for the young soldier.

"Hello, Charles," Buddy said, looking up from his work.

Charles sat down on a rickety chair across from Buddy. He unbuttoned his field jacket. "Things are quiet today. Headquarters was practically deserted.

"Coleman's locked up in his office," Charles continued. "Any idea what's going on?"

"Nope."

"Ames's death really hit him hard. It was all he could talk about when I saw him last night."

"He loved Lou," Buddy said softly.

"Yeah." Donnelly took a chocolate bar from his pocket. "I hope he finds out who did it."

Buddy nodded as he searched around for a clean corner of his rag.

"When you found him that day," Charles started hesitantly, "he definitely said he'd been shot by a sergeant? You're sure of that?"

Buddy's hands stopped moving. "Sure I'm sure. I saw the guy running away."

"Couldn't it have been an officer?"

"An officer?" Marks said. "How could it have been an officer? Ames said it wasn't. And the killer was still holding his M-1 rifle in his hands when I chased him."

"It couldn't have been a Tommy gun?" Donnelly knew a Tommy gun fired .45 slugs, the same as a .45 automatic pistol, and several officers carried them, including St. John, Turner, and, on occasion, the colonel. Although he doubted even Buddy could have confused a regular M-1 rifle with a Tommy gun, it was worth a try.

"No, it was an M-1. No doubt about that."

"He was wearing a cartridge belt?"

"Sure." Buddy put the boots on the floor next to the bed.

"Was Ames already on the ground when you found him?"

Buddy nodded.

"And I remember you said that you never actually went into the barn that day."

"He was already dead when I got back. I had to find the colonel."

"Quite right," said Charles. Rising to leave, he said, "Well, I'd better go see if I'm needed. Thanks for the chat."

Deep in thought, Charles started down the hallway towards his room. "Why did he lie?" he muttered.

"Why did who lie?"

Charles spun around.

"You were talking to yourself, old man. Army life getting to you?" St. John laughed. "Why did who lie?" he asked again.

"Oh, it's nothing," Donnelly answered.

"Listen, Charles. I got a message from the colonel. As soon as I get back, you and I are to report to him. Well, I'm back."

"Well, then, let's go."

Coleman rose anxiously from his chair as Donnelly and St. John entered the room. He saw that they were about to salute, and waved his hand indicating that it wasn't necessary.

By way of greeting, he said, "You got back just in time, Johnny. The regiment's going back on the line. We're moving out and up."

"You mean our happy, carefree life in the rear echelons is over?" asked St. John. He spoke casually. That he and Coleman were on good terms was obvious.

"It won't make much difference," said Charles. "We're across the Rhine. The Allied Armies are fanning out into Germany. And, besides, Johnny, we're in regimental headquarters, so our way of life won't change."

St. John raised his eyebrows. Coleman coughed. "You were away and missed the briefing. We're not just going back up," he said. "Whole division's being shifted into the Seventh Army."

"Why?" asked Charles.

"Because we're a tough outfit with a lot of combat experience."

"I thought that's why we were in the Third Army."

Coleman turned silent for a moment. Then he said, "On their western front, the Germans have several well-trained and well-equipped armies still in the field. And the strongest, best-equipped all seem to be right in the path of the U.S. Seventh Army. We think they'll fight to the end."

Donnelly looked at St. John.

"The Seventh Army's to the south of us," said John. "They, that is, we, are scheduled to cross the Main River, then head south into Bavaria. Nuremburg. Munich. All that."

"Damn!" exclaimed Donnelly. "Haven't we done enough fighting for one war? It's not fair!"

His outburst was spontaneous, and he regretted it as soon as the words were out of his mouth. "I'm sorry, sir," he said.

"It's all right, Charles. The war can't last much longer. Maybe another month at the most. But we've got to wrap it up. The Germans are going to fight to the last town, to the last ditch and to the last man, and we just have to go clean the bastards out. It happens we're part of one of the crack divisions in the United States Army, and that's why we get the tough ones. We can handle them."

The colonel walked over to a large map on the wall. Taking a pencil out of his pocket, he pointed: "Here's where we're going to relieve. As usual, I'll want Johnny to go ahead to pick out a good spot for our headquarters. Charles, you should go with him, but if your head still hurts..."

"No, sir! I can go."

"Fine," said Coleman. "You ought to start about 0500. I've assigned a radio communications Jeep to go with you, so you can keep in touch with me if necessary. Johnny knows the ropes. Any questions?"

The two officers shook their heads. Donnelly knew that St. John had done the same mission so many times he'd be able to fill in the blank spots for him.

As they turned to go, Coleman said, "Charles, there's one more thing I'd like to discuss with you. See you later, Johnny."

Donnelly watched St. John go. He wished that Coleman had assigned Johnny to this infernal investigation. After all, he was the intelligence officer. The whole damned thing was destined to do nothing but get everybody pissed off at Charles. And he didn't relish what he had to tell Coleman now, either.

"Sir," Charles started.

"I've just received word," cut in Coleman. "You and St. John are both being decorated with the Distinguished Service Cross for your actions at the Rhine."

"Gosh, sir. Thank you, sir." He knew that meant higher authorities had turned down the recommendation for the Medal of Honor and awarded him the next highest decoration, the D.S.C. Donnelly was pleased.

"Two officers from C.I.D. are coming up here tomorrow afternoon," continued Coleman. "I'd like you to talk to them when you get back. It will be the only chance you get before we move out. I've arranged for them to meet you here at 1600 hours."

"Yes, sir." Charles walked over to the window. The sun had disappeared behind a cloud, and the village suddenly seemed dour and forbidding. Collecting his thoughts, Charles turned back to Coleman. "Sir, I made some odd discoveries today that I think you should know about."

"Oh?"

"I found some evidence that strongly suggests that your nephew was not killed by one of our enlisted men."

"Charles, we've been over this. There is absolutely no chance that a German could have been inside our lines that day. Every blade of grass was checked." Coleman was interrupted by a knock on the door. Two soldiers came in with empty crates to load up Coleman's gear for the move out.

"Can you please wait? I'm afraid I'm in a meeting right now," Coleman said, in his usual friendly manner. He turned back to Donnelly. "You were saying?"

After the men retreated, Charles silently handed the clip pouch to Coleman.

"It's an ammunition pouch for a .45," Coleman said flatly.

"Yes, sir, I mentioned it earlier, before I'd given it much thought. It was clasped in Lou's hand but it didn't come from his own belt. I checked. Look at the back of it. I think he grabbed his killer by the waist as he fell to the ground."

Coleman looked at the back of the pouch and nodded. He turned it back over slowly. "Two snaps..." he said. "This is from an officer's belt."

"Marks specifically said that Lou was killed by a sergeant, not an officer," Donnelly said.

"Yes..."

"I thought he might have made a mistake, sir, so I questioned him this afternoon. He said he saw the killer running away; that he had a smoking M-1 rifle in his hands and was wearing a cartridge belt."

"He might have been telling the truth," Coleman said. "Perhaps Lou grabbed Marks as he fell. This could be Buddy's."

"I thought of that, sir. So I asked Buddy. He said he never went into the barn, that Lou was already lying on the ground when he found him. And there's more. I spoke to the medic who examined Ames. Your nephew was shot by a .45, not a rifle. I don't know why yet, but Buddy is lying to me."

"It certainly sounds that way," Coleman said, grim-faced.

"Sir, I'd like your permission to question him more fully, threaten him with a court-martial if he won't tell me the truth. There may be a simple explanation for all of this, but I need to get to the bottom of it, and that means forcing Buddy to talk. I'm sure he'll crack."

Coleman nodded thoughtfully. "Do whatever you need to do," he said, his voice filled with hard determination. He strode across the room, opened the door and said to the soldier on duty, "Go tell Lieutenant Marks I'd like to talk to him."

Several minutes later, the soldier returned, breathless. "Lieutenant Marks is out in the field, sir. Major Gonzalez-Rivera says he isn't due back until late tonight, sir."

"Of course." Coleman turned to Charles. "I sent him out to make sure all our companies received tonight's password and countersign. Since we're going back on the line, they've got to start taking that kind of crap more seriously. I'll radio him and tell him to get back here. As soon as he arrives, I'll let you know." Coleman slumped down in his chair and stared out at the deepening dusk. "Get some sleep, Charles."

Back in his small room, Charles put blankets over the windows and lit a kerosene lamp. Then he collapsed on the bed, tired and tense. He was leaving with St. John early in the morning, and he had to talk to Buddy before they left.

Charles looked at his watch. It might be hours before Buddy returned.

Well, he would just have to wait up for him. Lying on his back, staring up at the ceiling, Charles reviewed everything that he had learned. Was it really possible that Ames had been killed by a fellow officer? And if it were an officer, the equation changed radically.

The night before the crossing, Coleman had taken Ames with him to check the units going over. They split up, and Lou had stopped at Turner's company area, which was next to Charles's anti-tank platoon. Charles remembered the yelling and cursing that night. Lou and Turner had moved away from "B" company, not knowing Charles was so close-by. From the argument, Charles gathered that Turner had caught Ames trying on his captain's bars and was livid. "If you ever touch anything of mine again, you little prick, I'll fucking well blow your head off. And when we go into action, you damn well better cover your ass, 'cause the first chance I get, I'm gonna shove a bayonet up it and pull the trigger on my rifle. Got that? I don't give a happy fuck who your uncle is; as far as I'm concerned, you are a dead man!"

But now Donnelly's mind clouded with doubts. Turner had probably used the same menacing words to a lot of the officers he referred to as "college boys" or "sissy boys." Something in all of this didn't make sense. What had he missed? Charles sat up with a start. Of course. Turner and Marks. They were buddies. Turner was devoted to Marks. According to Johnny, old General Marks, then a major, had saved Turner's hide in the peacetime army of the '30s. According to St. John, Turner had beaten the hell out of a lieutenant over a girl, and Major Marks let him off with a slap on the wrist instead of twenty years hard labor. Yes! That was it. General Marks always claimed that sergeants were the backbone of the army, and as far as he was concerned, Turner was the best of the bunch.

Had Turner murdered Lou Ames and then asked Buddy Marks to cover for him? Were the pieces finally falling into place? Marks was the only one who was there. He was the only one who could identify the killer. And he was the only officer in the regiment who actually liked Paul Turner. But would Buddy cover for him?

6

The next morning, trucks jammed every road, advancing troops and supplies into Germany under a heavy grey sky pelting them with rain. Motor convoys stretched from the channel ports to the front lines like long columns of olive drab ants. Johnny's Jeep inched along in the middle of this massive traffic jam.

Marks had not returned. After being shaken awake by St. John, Charles had gone to Marks's room and found it was empty.

St. John skidded across a deep puddle almost sending Charles flying out of the Jeep.

"Didn't Coleman tell you to take a driver?" asked Charles irritably.

John shrugged, looking back to make sure the communications Jeep still followed him. "I like to do my own driving. Sometimes I have to go where the climate's not very healthy. You know, steel flying all over the place. I feel better taking my chances alone."

Gradually, the number of vehicles on the rutted road began to thin out, and the Jeep made better time. John stuck his head out to see if they could safely pass the big trucks lumbering along in convoy.

Even though Donnelly was pretty sure what had happened in the barn on the day of the murders, he decided to verify as many details as he could. And Johnny could be a vast fountain of information. He kept his ears and eyes open. He was a checker and a double-checker. He was the one who'd told him about Turner and Marks's father. Intelligence sources, he supposed.

"Johnny," Charles began casually, "what kind of relationship did Buddy have with Lou Ames?"

"Same as the rest of us," St. John said. He saw a break in the traffic and shot ahead, swerving into the middle of the convoy where debris narrowed the road, before shooting ahead again.

Donnelly waited for more but St. John kept quiet. "Listen, Johnny, Ames and I never had much contact. I hardly knew the guy. So I need to talk to someone who was his friend." Donnelly pressed on. "Usually the friends know who the enemies are."

St. John hesitated before answering. "I'd say we all kept our distance from Ames. He really didn't have any friends.... Ah hell, Charles, everybody hated the son of a bitch. He was nothing but a miserable little coward."

"Is that why no one will talk to me about him? I'm getting the cold shoulder from everybody."

"Look, Charles," St. John said, pressing down on the accelerator, "Ames was obviously not the self-sacrificing hero that Coleman thinks he was. But Coleman's tops. We all love and admire him, so nobody wants to say anything against his despicable nephew. Coleman adored that kid."

The traffic appeared more warlike as they moved closer to the front. Artillery pieces, tanks, truckloads of infantry. The wind was at their backs or they would have heard the firing by now.

"I can tell you one thing," Johnny said thoughtfully. "But you didn't hear it from me, understood?"

"You have my word."

"As far as I can remember, the only time Coleman ever got angry with Ames, it was about Buddy."

"What happened?" Donnelly asked.

"Buddy decked him with one punch. Can you imagine that? Buddy, the titmouse?"

Charles shook his head. "Did Ames press charges? You can't just haul off and slug another officer like that."

John laughed. "Do you think Coleman would let him do that? You're crazy. We all know Buddy is the son of old General Marks. And I mean old four star General Marks. You don't suppose Larry Coleman's going to let anything spoil his relationship there, do you? He gave Ames hell and told him never to talk to Buddy like that again. That's all he did. Anyway it was the only time I ever saw Coleman get angry with Lou."

"I wonder what Ames did to Marks," Charles said thoughtfully.

John remained silent for a moment. Then, he said, "Look, Charles, I promised on my word of honor to Buddy that I'd never tell. But I know."

"Then, for God's sake tell me."

"It's a long story, Charles. It was a black night in the fall of '44. Buddy was driving through a gusty rainstorm. Ames was with him. They passed countless clumps of American soldiers sleeping beside the road. The men were on rest leave from the front and obviously had been drinking. The road was covered by branches blown from the trees and, with the Jeep's blackout lights on, it was particularly hard to see what lay ahead. From time to time they hit piles of debris, and the Jeep would lurch, tossing Marks and Ames off their seats. Buddy wanted to drive more slowly, but Ames kept urging him to go faster. Said he was tired and wanted to get to bed. When an old army raincoat suddenly appeared in their way, Buddy had not been able to stop, and had simply run over it with a jolt.

'What was that?' Buddy asked Ames, slowing the Jeep.

'Nothing,' Ames replied. 'More debris.'

'It might have been a man,' said Buddy. 'Let's go back and see.'

'Oh, for the love of Mike, it was just another piece of wood. I saw it. Now let's get going. I want to get to bed.'

"They drove on despite Buddy's misgivings," St. John shouted to be heard over the roar and the growl of the trucks he passed. "The next day Buddy overheard the men talking. Some poor G.I. had fallen asleep in the road and been run over. He'd survived for a while, until finally a group of drunken soldiers had stumbled on him and taken him to the aid station. But it had been too late. He had lost too much blood. Buddy was sick about it. He told Ames he was going to go to Colonel Coleman and turn himself in and he thought Ames should do the same. Once again, Ames talked him out of it. He pointed out that the scandal would kill Buddy's father. And, besides, how did they know it was their Jeep that ran over the man. He was sure that they had hit a log. Somebody else had run over the G.I. And so, the two men agreed never to mention the matter again.

"Then one day, after the Battle of the Bulge, the two headquarters lieutenants got into an argument. Ames was boasting about his heroism, now that he had finally gotten a chance to prove himself in battle.

'You didn't do anything,' Buddy insisted. 'You stayed so far down in your foxhole, you didn't even know what was going on.'

'That's a lie!' Ames shot back. 'I killed a lot of Germans. Everybody knows that...'

'Nobody saw you kill anybody. You just say you did, but that doesn't make it so.'

'Well, that still makes me a better man than you. The only man you ever killed was a G.I. and he was asleep at the time...'

"That's when Buddy knocked Ames on his ass. He was about to really maul Ames, when several men rushed over to pull him away. Ames was stunned and took several seconds to recover his wits. He got up slowly, glared at Buddy and stalked off. From that moment on Buddy has hated Lou Ames with a passion. A punch on the jaw didn't settle the score. Buddy Marks told me he'd promised himself that he would get even with Lou Ames—somehow, somewhere. Now you know as much as I do about the 'slugging' incident."

It took Charles a moment to digest the tale Johnny had just told him. Then, he asked, "Did Marks really tell you about this?"

"I got it from the horse's mouth, old friend. From Buddy Marks, himself."

"Well," Charles said finally, "I guess that does it. No more mystery. Now we know the reason Buddy lied. He shot Ames."

"Not so fast, Charles. How about the rape? Can you, by the farthest stretch of your imagination, picture Buddy raping a girl?"

Charles had to shake his head. Now he was really confused.

"Buddy despised Ames for a specific reason. The rest of us despised him on general principles. He was nasty, the kind of kid who never should have been an officer. He once busted a regular army sergeant for getting back half an hour late from his wedding furlough. He'd put men on report for not saluting; he'd chew out a sergeant in front of his men. After the Bulge, when the regiment went into reserve to replace casualties and equipment, he canceled all leaves for the men of 'A' Company because he thought one of them had taken his bottle of Scotch, remember? You were with us then. And when it turned up later inside his own sleeping bag, it was too late to send the men on leave. Quite a few of the enlisted men would have been happy to knock off the little prick. On top of which, he cheated me at poker. Now that's a hanging offense."

"Were you glad when you heard he'd been killed?"

"The man was no good! When he came across me at the minefield where Sauter got it, he refused to help me. I was desperate. I begged him. But he ran off and left me alone to face forty Germans. I almost shot him then and there."

Charles said thoughtfully, "I guess it doesn't matter what Ames's killer felt about him. Whoever murdered Ames did it because Lou caught him raping the girl. The killer didn't need any other motive."

"Don't be naive, Charles."

"What do you mean?"

"Rape is rare. In the infrequent case where some G.I. does commit rape, he hangs, and you can count on it. If you or I caught somebody raping a girl, we'd have him locked up until he was court-martialed and hanged. We'd do that just as sure as hell. But we wouldn't just haul off and shoot him. Ames wouldn't have shot the rapist, either, and the rapist knew that. Lou didn't even have his gun drawn, for Pete's sake. No, whoever killed Ames did it because he wanted to. He had probably been waiting a long time for the right moment."

"At least that narrows down the field a bit," Charles said, digesting what Johnny had said.

"I wouldn't count on it. Nobody had a reason not to kill Lou Ames." St. John pulled off the road into a small path that headed into the woods.

"Been here before?" asked Charles.

"No. But I memorized the map before we left. The C.P. of the outfit we're relieving should be in these woods."

Charles looked behind them. The radio Jeep was right there where it should be. The terrain was rough and the Jeep pitched and rolled like a small boat in an Atlantic storm. Donnelly held on for dear life.

An American soldier stepped into the Jeep's path. He held his M-1 rifle carelessly at his hip, its barrel aimed directly at St. John. Passwords were exchanged, and Johnny told the guard what his mission was. The man smiled and saluted. "About a hundred yards farther on, sir," he said. "You'll see a bunch of G.I.'s and some vehicles."

As soon as they'd gone the hundred yards, they came to a clearing where half a dozen large trucks and several Jeeps were parked. After getting out of their Jeep and talking to the colonel and several other officers, John asked about the town he and Donnelly had just passed through. The colonel said he thought it was dangerous to set up a C.P. in an exposed town. Charles sized him up. He was obviously not an experienced commander, probably a political-type officer. John thanked him, and got back into the Jeep.

"We'll relieve them after sundown," said St. John. "In the meantime, I'll take a look at that town. I usually know what Colonel Coleman likes."

After they started off, with the radio Jeep right behind them, Charles said, "We didn't even inspect their positions."

"We've both seen fox holes before. Besides, we won't be here long. Coleman'll knock hell out of those Krauts up there, and away we'll go. The reason we're relieving this other outfit is that they've been shot up pretty badly and are coming out of the line to go into reserve. They'll get some new equipment and infantry replacements, then go back. Just like us."

✪

On the outskirts of another German village, several miles away, Buddy Marks lay in a field staring up at the sky. He'd returned late the night before, slept fitfully for a couple of hours, then gotten up long before dawn and taken off again. He wanted to be alone to think things through. But the colonel would be waiting for him. Buddy sighed. He closed his eyes. He lay quietly for just a few more moments. He gazed out at the sky. It looked like it was raining in the distance.

Then he got to his feet.

✪

When Donnelly and St. John returned, two C.I.D. officers were waiting to confer with each one separately in an out-of-the-way tent guarded by armed Military Police, as arranged by Colonel Coleman the preceding day. Charles entered the tent first and saluted the major in charge.

"You and two other officers brought back the bodies of Lieutenant Ames and the girl," said the major without preamble.

"Yes, sir."

"Where were they? That is, what area of the barn?"

"She was in the back, and Lieutenant Ames was beside the front door."

"Do you know who killed them?" asked the major.

"No, sir. I assume the rapist did, but I don't know—"

"I see," said the major. "Do you have any information to give us?"

"No, sir. That is, sir, as you know, Lieutenant Ames was Colonel Coleman's nephew, and the colonel put me in charge of trying to find out what happened at the barn, but I assume your unit will take over the investigation from now on, and I—"

"Wrong, Lieutenant. Carry on." The major stood, signifying the interview was over. They exchanged salutes, and that was that.

As far as Charles was concerned, his conference with them regarding Ames was cursory and most unsatisfactory. They didn't seem to expect to solve the murder. By now, John had entered the tent, and Charles waited for him to come out.

He wasn't in the tent long, either.

"How did it go?" asked Charles.

"Short and sweet," replied John. " They're not really interested. The trail is cold and enlisted men shoot their officers fairly frequently it seems."

However, to Donnelly's great surprise, the area seemed to be crawling with Counter Intelligence officers. They were waiting for Charles and Johnny and summoned them into their tent, also guarded by M.P.'s, but even farther away from the headquarters. Charles gulped as he saluted the light colonel in charge.

To Donnelly, this officer seemed more courteous than the C.I.D. major. He nodded at St. John and extended his hand and shook Charles's. "Welcome, Lieutenant. Appreciate your coming."

"Thank you, sir."

"Will you please describe to me exactly where you found the murdered girl?"

"Yes, sir. She was lying in the straw at the far end of the barn."

"Can you describe her condition?"

"Yes, sir," replied Charles, hesitantly. "Her clothes were ripped off, and her throat was slashed. There was blood all over the straw around her head."

"Anything else?"

"It appeared she was waiting for somebody, sir."

"Why do you say that, Lieutenant?"

"She'd brought food to the barn. I'd guess something to eat while she waited, sir."

The colonel nodded. "Very good, Lieutenant," he said. "You can go now."

As Charles saluted, the colonel addressed St. John. "Come sit down, Captain," he said.

St. John didn't appear until an hour and a half after Charles left. They must really be grilling him, thought Charles. He realized the intelligence officer hadn't asked him anything about Ames. Just the girl. Odd.

As it became obvious that St. John would be in the tent awhile, Charles thought of his father. The Judge had always been aloof and formal with him. But after the Third Army's dash across France during the summer of '44, he received a letter from his dad telling him how proud he was of him and what a great job he and his fellow soldiers were doing. That was the closest thing to praise he'd received from his father, whom he'd tried to please all his life without any visible success. However, after the Battle of the Bulge, Charles received the letter he carried in his shirt pocket all the time. It read, in part: "During that awful German winter offensive, I feared for your safety twenty-four hours a day. I worried about you, son, in that maelstrom of carnage, and I couldn't help you in any way. The frustration was terrible, and I trembled whenever I saw a Western Union telegram being delivered. I want you to know, son, that I love you very much and pray for you every day." Charles knew that letter by heart.

When John came out of the tent, Charles stood nearby. "Why in the name of God did they keep you so long?" he demanded. "I was out of there in five minutes, but you were inside for hours."

"Oh, they just liked me." St. John smiled. "No, Charles, actually I knew Colonel Smithen before. We're friends and simply caught up with each other. Told a few jokes, reminisced about old times, the usual stuff."

"Baloney."

"Why? I'm the intelligence officer of this regiment. Smithen heads a real intelligence unit. It's natural for us to know each other. Do you know any lawyers who don't know other lawyers? Come on, Charles, get a grip on yourself."

Somebody had picked up Donnelly's mail for him. There was a letter from his mother and one from his brother, David. He read David's first. The gist of it was that David had met a wonderful girl. Unfortunately, mother didn't approve, but David put that down to the fact the girl was from the wrong part of town and worked as a dancer in a nightclub. But, said David, it was her soul that attracted him, and he intended to marry her as soon as the war was over.

Charles shook his head slowly, trying to decide how he was going to answer his nutty brother. He shrugged. Maybe the girl was all right.

His mother's letter started out with the good news that his father had won appointment to the Federal Appeals Court and was overwhelmingly happy. Charles smiled. Reading on, his mother wrote: Oh, your friend Muffy had a little boy and is very happy, even though she and her husband live in New York. Charles laughed out loud. He knew what his mother meant, but it came out so amusingly. Anyway, she continued, David's girlfriend is moving to California with her show, so that fixes that. David is still in basic training in Florida and will go to another camp when he finishes. Shaking his head, Charles stood up. He'll be going overseas as an infantry replacement, he thought. God, I hope this war ends soon.

"Hurry up," shouted Buddy Marks as St. John's Jeep slid to a stop after he had finished with the Criminal Investigations and

Counter Intelligence officers. By now, it was late in the afternoon, still overcast, still raining sporadically. The air was chilly.

"Hurry up for what?" asked Johnny.

"There's a quartermaster shower unit in town. The line companies have all gone through, and now it's our turn. Cannon Company and Antitank are ahead of us, but that's all. Let's go."

Donnelly idly wondered if Coleman had spoken to Buddy about their new-found suspicions that an officer had killed Ames. Marks seemed in high spirits so perhaps the misunderstanding was cleared up.

As he headed for the showers, Charles tried to figure out why the Counter Intelligence people were so interested. It didn't make any sense.

When infantry units went into a quartermaster shower, which wasn't often, they left all their dirty, battle-stained clothing at the entrance in piles. Field jackets in one pile, trousers in another, shirts, underwear, long johns, socks, even handkerchiefs. When they came out at the other end of the showers, they picked out clean but unpressed replacement uniforms, which had been left just as filthy as theirs by the preceding unit, then laundered to distribute to the next unit to shower.

As Charles Donnelly emptied the pockets of his trousers, he stared dumbly at the strip of olive drab cloth. He dreaded the chore of surreptitiously checking the field jackets of each officer.

At the other end of the showers, he hurried into his clean uniform and dashed out to the entrance of the shower tent. Suddenly Charles realized the chore could be accomplished with ease. The piles of dirty uniforms were still there. A quartermaster sergeant stood nearby. "Are these all from Headquarters Company?" asked Charles, motioning towards the piles.

The man nodded.

Charles made for the pile of field jackets. He started sorting through them, examining each one with care. Nothing. He was halfway through the pile when his eye caught sight of the lower half of a field jacket sleeve hanging out of the pile of shirts. He pulled it free and turned it over. He could tell by the tiny holes where the insignia had been pinned that it was an officer's jacket. On the back of the jacket a thin strip of fabric had been ripped away. Donnelly positioned his piece of cloth over the tear. It was a match—exact and unmistakable. Charles's heart raced. He felt excited. Finally a break. Then, he sucked in his breath. No, he thought. Not Buddy. This isn't the way I wanted it to end.

The quartermaster put up an argument, but, in the end, Charles Donnelly walked away with the dirty field jacket. As he trudged back to the building that served as the home and office to the regiment, his brow was furrowed in concern. He half-heartedly returned the salutes of the enlisted men who passed him, but he was preoccupied with the jacket and the conclusion to which it led him. The company has only one officer who was large enough to wear that jacket—Buddy Marks. And, since the piece came from Buddy's jacket, it meant that Buddy had been inside the barn around the time of the murder. He certainly had not stood any-where near the door when he went in with Johnny and me. So, he'd lied. Lied to everybody about not entering the barn when Lou was killed. Why would he have lied about that unless he was the murderer. But would Buddy Marks rape a girl? Never. Charles felt more confused than ever.

"Colonel Coleman?" Donnelly said to the guard at Coleman's door.

"Sorry, sir. The colonel's not in. We're moving up, sir, and he's with the line companies, getting them started."

"We should've moved out by now," said Donnelly. "We told those guys we'd relieve them at nightfall."

"Change in plans, sir."

Donnelly smiled. "He wanted to take a shower, just like everybody else, you mean?"

The man grinned back at Charles and nodded. "The colonel said that 'just before dawn' was as good a time as any, sir."

"Well, since you'll be here guarding the door, I'll leave this inside the colonel's office, Okay?" said Donnelly, opening the door and gently placing the jacket on the colonel's desk, noting that the guard eyed his every move. "Tell him I'll explain what it's all about when he gets back."

Charles Donnelly asked a half-dozen men whether they'd seen Lieutenant Marks since leaving the showers. No one had. Despite the darkness, Charles headed into the woods, hoping he'd find Buddy. The young soldier seemed to enjoy communing with nature. As he headed to the edge of town, someone shouted, "Be careful, Lieutenant. Might be Jerries around." He waved at his unknown advisers. "Watch out for mines, sir!"

Again, Charles waved and shouted, "Thanks. I will."

Softly, he called, "Buddy? Buddy, are you there?"

No reply.

He wasn't at headquarters. Nobody had seen him. He wouldn't have moved up with a rifle company. No. He'd wait and move with everyone else. So, where in the hell could he be? He was away all night last night, too. Hey, maybe he found a girl somewhere around here. Yes. Dammit, why hadn't he thought of that? Of course.

Charles felt much better as he made his way back through the tall trees towards his regiment. He rubbed his hands together with glee. That rascal, he mused. Imagine. Buddy Marks, the inept, making out with a beautiful German girl right under their noses. Some guys were just plain lucky. Then, without warning, he spotted the gentle giant. He was hanging by his neck from a stout bough, swaying slightly as a breeze wafted through the leaves.

Half an hour later, a group of men from the regiment gathered around the body hanging from the tree. Buddy's uniform was neat except that the collar had been pulled back slightly to allow the noose to fit around his neck without obstruction. His neck didn't look like it had broken, so Charles imagined Buddy died from strangulation. There was no helmet, either on Marks or anywhere nearby, and Charles had had a chance to look around before the others arrived. He could hardly bring himself to look at Buddy's now mottled face.

Coleman shook his head. "I guess we've found our murderer," he said sadly.

"Hanged himself with a half inch rope," commented a sergeant. "Tied one end around the limb of a tree, the other around his neck."

"Where the hell did Buddy get a half inch rope?" Coleman asked.

The supply sergeant, a man named Dickins, answered guiltily, "I issued it to him, sir. He said he wanted it for Lieutenant Donnelly."

Charles stood there too dumbstruck to say anything.

"Why Donnelly?" asked Coleman.

"He didn't say, sir." Dickins shivered slightly.

"Charles, did you send Buddy to get this rope?"

"You know perfectly well I didn't. You're getting upset, sir. It's obvious Buddy used me as an excuse to cover the real reason he wanted to draw the rope. He could have used you just as well, or Johnny, or anybody."

Coleman nodded, though Donnelly wondered if a cloud of suspicion now hung over his head.

Donnelly asked Coleman, "Did you ever reach Marks last night, sir? Did he know you were looking for him?"

"Yes. I radioed him. Told him I needed to question him about Lou. He sounded a bit odd, but then that didn't surprise me after our conversation. When he didn't come back, I sent Turner to look for him. But he came back empty-handed. Buddy didn't turn up until this afternoon."

"Yes, I saw him at the showers," said Charles.

"So does this mean you think Buddy killed Lou?" asked Johnny, who had been one of the first men on the scene.

"Yes," Coleman sighed, "though of all the men in this army, Buddy is the one man I would have thought incapable of such an act. It is hard to know what to think. My nephew's death has been avenged, and yet I don't feel glad."

Charles thought a moment. "I wonder why."

"Why what?"

"Why Buddy killed Ames."

"And the girl," added St. John.

Coleman shrugged sadly. "We'll never know, will we?"

By now, three enlisted men struggled to get the body down; it was heavy, and the ground was slippery after the heavy rainfall. Coleman and Donnelly watched uncomfortably, as two soldiers supported Buddy's weight and another perched on the tree branch trying to loosen the rope.

Poor, awkward Buddy. Charles couldn't understand how he could be a killer—or a rapist. In death Buddy looked even larger than he had in life. Feeling rather foolish for playing the detective in front of the colonel, Charles felt Buddy's hand. It was still warm. "He must have killed himself this evening," Charles said slowly. "I wonder why he waited."

"Strange," Coleman agreed. "Perhaps he planned to go AWOL after I spoke to him and then realized that he wouldn't get very far."

"When you spoke to him he was miles from here. Yet he came back to headquarters. I think he meant to turn himself in but lost his nerve."

"Possibly. Well, I'd better get in touch with C.I.D.," Coleman said gruffly. "Tell them to forget it."

"Does this mean I'm off the case, sir?"

"Yes. You did a fine job, Donnelly. I'm just sorry it turned out the way it did. I'd appreciate it if you'd stay and oversee things a bit."

Charles nodded absently, gazing at the corpse. Something struck him as odd. "Sir. Look at his boots."

Coleman glanced at Buddy's boots, buffed as usual as if he'd just left headquarters or stepped out of a Jeep.

"What about them?"

"They're clean. Even the soles don't have any mud on them."

"Yes?"

Charles hesitated, not really wanting to go in the direction his logic was leading him. "Well, sir, at headquarters it's dry, but here it's been raining. The ground all around here is extremely wet and muddy. How did Buddy get here from headquarters without getting his boots covered with mud?"

This gave Coleman pause. He frowned, stared at Buddy, then at the sea of mud around them. "I don't know Charles, but he did, didn't he?"

"Maybe someone else..." Charles could take the thought no further, knowing it would anger his already over-burdened commander.

Coleman narrowed his eyes. "Someone else what? Killed him and then hanged him from the tree?"

"Yes, sir."

To Charles's surprise, Coleman seemed to consider the possibility.

"But Charles, how on earth would anyone get a great lump like Buddy into a tree? Whoever it was would have to be a man of superhuman strength, don't you think?"

As if to demonstrate the truth of Coleman's statement, the soldier in the tree finally cut the noose, and his two comrades collapsed under the sudden weight of the corpse, which hit the ground with a dull thud. The soldiers, cursing, had to squirm out from beneath the body.

Charles was relieved to have his doubts scotched. "Yes, sir, of course, you're right. It's impossible; no one could lift him up there."

Coleman rubbed his chin and said, "Unless you're suggesting a conspiracy. Three or four men might have done it."

"That doesn't seem very likely," Donnelly answered. "Everyone loved Buddy."

"Yes, you're right. It doesn't seem very likely. But, Charles, give it some thought. I must be off." And with that, Coleman nodded at Charles and walked away.

Charles remained to supervise the removal of the body. A Jeep rolled in, and the soldiers struggled to get Marks's enormous body in.

The Jeep's driver got out and stood by.

"Don't just stand there," snapped Charles, "help us."

"Yes, sir. Sorry, sir," said the driver, reluctantly taking hold of a lifeless arm. "You know, sir, if you'd waited, I could've driven right up underneath him. Then you could have just cut him down and he'd have dropped in the back nice and easy like a bale of cotton."

Charles thought that over. The driver was right, they could have done just that... or someone else might have done exactly the reverse to get Buddy into the tree. First, though, he'd have had to knock him out or kill him, put him in a Jeep, drive out here, put the rope around his neck, attach a slipknot to the branch, heave the body up by pulling on the rope until Buddy was almost standing in the Jeep, then drive off and leave him hanging. It was possible, and it wouldn't be difficult.

Looking closely, Charles could just make out a faint set of tire marks leading away towards the far pasture. Charles climbed up into the Jeep and uncovered Buddy's body. He could see no obvious wound. No bullet mark or cut.

"Give me a hand with this, would you?" he asked one of the soldiers. They turned the body onto its front. On the back of Buddy's head Charles found a large bump. It looked as if he'd been hit hard with a heavy object.

"Guess his head hit the ground when we cut him down, huh, sir?"

"Guess so," Charles said, choosing not to remind the young G.I. that it was he who had broken Buddy's fall.

Charles shook his head slowly. A few moments ago, he'd been sure Buddy was the man. First, he lied about the enlisted man and the rifle. Second, that piece of cloth he found in the barn came off a field jacket so large it could only have fit Marks. Third, he had a motive: he violently hated Ames. And fourth, he hanged himself. But number four didn't hold up under scrutiny. And if he didn't hang himself, the other three facts became meaningless.

"Stop," Donnelly shouted to the driver just as the Jeep was pulling out. "Wait, I want to look at Marks's web belt."

The regiment was just leaving to move toward the new line, when the Jeep carrying Marks's body arrived at headquarters. Charles charged up the stairs and ran into Coleman's office without knocking.

"Sir," he said breathlessly.

"Yes?" It was Gonzalez-Rivera, standing behind the door, rolling up some maps.

"Oh. Where's the colonel?"

"He's gone on ahead. Can I help you with something, Lieutenant?"

"No, I..."

"I heard about Marks. What a shame."

"Yes. He was a good kid."

"Oh?" Gonzalez-Rivera raised an eyebrow. "How can you say that?" He bent down to pick up some papers that had fallen to the ground. "Good kid, indeed. I heard he was our murderer."

"Sir?"

"Coleman says that your secret little investigation flushed Marks out as our mystery killer."

"You know about it?"

Gonzalez-Rivera nodded. "Coleman thinks his conscience got to him."

"If he did kill Ames, he was bound to hang anyway," Charles said defensively.

Gonzalez-Rivera looked at him sharply. "If?"

Donnelly thought it best not to elaborate. He shrugged.

"It seems you've developed a taste for detective work," Gonzalez-Rivera said.

"As a matter of fact, yes. It sure beats fighting Tiger tanks with nothing but a little 57 mm popgun."

The major smiled for the first time since Charles had known him. "Okay," he said. "You're right about that. But, Lieutenant, if I may try to be helpful, please be careful. Watch your back and don't start prying too deeply into other people's business. You'll just make them upset and uncooperative."

Donnelly smiled back at the major. "Thank you, sir."

Gonzalez-Rivera, with a casual wave, said, "Well, I must be running. Keep safe."

Donnelly watched him disappear down the corridor. Was that a worried frown he detected on the Major's face?

Donnelly caught up with Coleman in the town that he and St. John had scouted the previous morning. It seemed clear from Coleman's choice of a headquarters, a run-down tavern that looked like it might collapse, that Coleman did not plan to stay for more than a few nights.

Outside the tavern, a hot meal of liberated beef was being served up, and a long line of men had formed. Donnelly waved to Russo and Novak without stopping. He had to get this conversation over with quickly or he'd lose out on some decent grub and it would be yet another night of canned K ration pork loaf and powdered bouillon.

The interior of the tavern, dank and badly lit, stank of yeast and sweat. Coleman sat alone in an upstairs room, planning tomorrow's fighting. The combat units were moving east toward the Main River.

He acknowledged Charles with a quick nod. "Lieutenant."

"Sir, I'm sorry to bother you, but I think it's important."

"Well, what is it?" Coleman said resignedly.

Coleman listened quietly as Charles described his findings in the orchard. At the end, Coleman said, "I hate to admit it, but you may be right. Though a bump on the head and tire tracks are very circumstantial."

"Yes, sir. But what about the belt? He was still wearing his web belt, and I took a long, hard look at it. If he was the one who killed Lou, then his belt would have been missing a metal ring. It wasn't."

Coleman nodded thoughtfully. "I suppose he could have changed belts, of course."

"I think Buddy was protecting someone. He must have seen something. When I asked him if it had been an officer who killed Ames, I was still shooting in the dark. I really had no idea. But now I think that I must have hit the nail on the head. Whoever killed Marks did it because he thought Buddy was going to crack when we questioned him again." Donnelly paused. "Who knew that you were looking for Buddy?"

Coleman shook his head with frustration. "I'm afraid I put the word out to just about everyone."

"That doesn't narrow it down much."

"It certainly doesn't."

"So we're back to square one. The only way we'll find out who murdered Marks and Ames is by going back to Ames's killing. I have to find out which officers were in the vicinity of the barn and away from their men during the fighting at the Rhine."

"I can save you the trouble. I can tell you who was in the area that morning: you, me, Turner, Sauter, St. John, Marks, Gonzalez-Rivera, and Lou." Coleman thought for moment. "Sauter, Ames, and Marks are dead. That leaves five officers."

"Yes, sir."

"And, Charles, be careful. I'm afraid that the number might get even smaller before we're through. So, please don't turn your back to anybody on a dark night."

"The major gave me the same advice. But I think I can take care of myself."

"I imagine that's what Buddy thought, too."

Downstairs, Paul Turner sat on an empty wooden keg next to the bar, cleaning his .45 pistol. He got up when he saw Donnelly, and stood in front of the staircase, blocking Charles's exit.

"Excuse me, Captain Turner."

"You ain't going nowhere, Lieutenant."

"Is there a problem, Captain?"

"Yeah. And you're it."

Charles tried to push past Turner. The man had been drinking, and was clearly itching for a fight. An empty bottle of schnapps sat on the bar.

Turner shoved him backwards. "Buddy didn't hang himself. He was killed."

"What are you saying?" Charles asked carefully.

"I'm saying Buddy was murdered," Turner shouted. "And I think you did it."

"You're nuts. Marks was found hanging from a tree, Turner."

"That's what they say. They also say he killed Lou Ames—and that it was you sticking your nose in everybody else's friggin' business that pushed him over the edge."

"Coleman asked me to investigate. I didn't have a choice."

"Marks never killed nobody, you idiot, not even a Kraut. The kid had a heart of gold. I don't give a damn who killed Lou Ames, and neither does anybody else. He was an asshole and deserved to die. But Buddy Marks was my friend. I say your goddam fucking questions are what killed him."

Donnelly decided the best form of defense was attack. "Why did you hate Ames so much, Captain?"

Turner turned a deeper shade of purple and a mean glint appeared in his eyes. "You saying I killed him?"

Donnelly knew better than to back down now. He tried to sound tougher than he felt. "Maybe. Did you?"

It was Turner who backed off slightly. "What? For God's sake, Donnelly, I suppose you think I killed Buddy as well!" There was a definite hint of bluster in his voice now.

Charles, thinking on his feet, decided to push a little more. "Captain, I heard you threaten Ames once."

"That's a crock of shit, Lieutenant. I never threatened Ames."

"If I remember correctly, the exact words were, 'You are a dead man.'"

Turner looked confused so Donnelly elucidated. "It was the night he tried on your captain's bars. You were cussing—"

Turner laughed abruptly. "Donnelly, you really take the cake. First, you eavesdrop on one little fight I had with that little piss-ant and then decide I'm the murderer. Gee, Lieutenant, you're a regular Sherlock Holmes."

Donnelly ignored the insult. "Captain, you were the one who went to look for him last night. You could easily have—"

"You little shit! I oughta—" Turner's eyes bulged.

"You ought to what? Hang me?"

Turner obviously realized through his drunken haze that he was making trouble for himself. "Screw you, Sherlock," he muttered, and staggered away. Donnelly watched him go. He found to his mild shame that Gonzalez-Rivera was right; he was beginning to enjoy being a detective.

7

Donnelly spent the next morning chasing down various soldiers who had participated in Task Force Coleman. Many of the men had already been sent ahead towards the River Main, but by high noon he had managed to find out much of what he needed to know. Some of the men thought Gonzalez-Rivera might have disappeared shortly after he had landed on the eastern bank of the Rhine. He had been seen heading down to the aid station, but none of the medics remembered seeing him there. Still, they hastened to say, there had been so many wounded that morning, they might not have noticed the major. He was probably checking the communications wires, thought Charles.

Besides Gonzalez-Rivera, that left Paul Turner. And St. John, of course.

Donnelly was heading down to find some of the men from King Company when he saw Joe Ainsley strolling toward the officers' mess. Ainsley had been Turner's executive officer during the Rhine crossing.

"Ainsley," Donnelly ran to catch up with him.

By now it seemed that every soldier this side of Berlin knew that Donnelly was playing detective; Ainsley took one look at him, waved his hand as if to say, 'no comment,' and picked up his pace.

"Lieutenant," said Donnelly, trying to put a hint of the policeman in his tone, "I need a moment of your time."

Ainsley stopped reluctantly. "Sir, I'm in a hurry, as you may have noticed."

"Won't take a minute. Tell me, Ainsley, you were with Turner on the twenty-first, weren't you?"

"Yes," Ainsley said tersely.

"All through the day?"

Ainsley nodded.

Donnelly persisted. "Was there any time at all when you lost sight of him?"

"Listen, sir," said Ainsley with a touch of anger in his voice, "I know what you're trying to do. And it won't work. Not with me. Captain Turner is a fine officer and a good man and I'm not going to say anything that could get him into trouble, is that understood?"

"He's not in any trouble."

"Then why am I standing here getting grilled by you?"

Donnelly smiled disarmingly. "Because two of our soldiers and a young German girl have been murdered. Do you like to see people get away with murder?"

"Turner's not a murderer."

"I never said he was. So tell me, please, was there any time on the twenty-first when you lost sight of Turner?"

Ainsley shifted his feet. "He left briefly to do some recon. Normal stuff. The captain does it all the time." Then he added sharply, "I believe, Lieutenant, it is part of his job."

"And what time did he leave?" Donnelly asked.

"I don't know."

"Why's that, Lieutenant? I see you wear a watch."

"Because," Ainsley said, raising his voice, "I'm sick of your questions. Now, if you'll excuse me, this conversation is over."

"Very well, Ainsley. Thank you."

Ainsley stalked off to the mess, and Charles silently cursed himself for his lack of guile. Detectives in books and films always seemed to manage such scenes with more tact and a great deal more success. But he sensed that Ainsley wasn't telling the whole truth. Something was being held back.

Finally, after an hour of diligent searching, Donnelly found an enlisted man in Turner's company, drunk, and in need of more booze. Johnson, a big Minnesota butcher, slumped in the corner of a derelict building, an empty bottle rolling round at his feet. A half pint of whiskey that Donnelly had been hoarding turned him into Johnson's friend for life.

"On the day of the crossing," Johnson said, taking a swig, "we held off a heavy German attack right after we dug foxholes along the banks of this shallow creek, see. When the Germans hauled ass, we cheered. That's when Lieutenant Ames showed up and gave Captain Turner hell. Said his troop dispositions stank. Did it right in front of us enlisted men.

"He told Captain Turner that he didn't have the brains to be commanding us," Johnson remembered with a drunken smile. "And, oh baby, did that piss the captain off. He told Ames to get his ass out in front of our foxhole line so he could get a better look. We all had a good laugh at that. But Ames, he got real mad. As he left, he shook his fist at the captain and said he would have him court-martialed. That brought even more catcalls."

"What did Turner do then?" Charles probed.

"He just laughed." As an afterthought Johnson said, "But later, when he left us to go scout around, Captain Turner told us, 'If that little chickenshit prick Ames shows up again, shoot him.' We probably would have, too." Johnson laughed, then chugged the rest of the whisky.

So Turner had left his troops, Donnelly thought. Both Ainsley and Johnson confirmed it, although Ainsley was not specific about the time Turner was away. More than that, Turner had specifically said that he wanted Ames dead—twice! The circle was narrowing. Four down, one to go. St. John. Nonsense, of course, but he had to check on all five.

As he trudged back toward headquarters, Charles once again took stock. Out of the five officers, everyone but Gonzalez-Rivera and Turner had an alibi. And then there was Johnny. He had been working alone that day, doing reconnaissance, and his actions could not be accounted for by anyone. And yet… Johnny was his best friend; surely he was incapable of such an act.

Only three officers had the opportunity to murder Ames. But how could he possibly discover which one it was? There were no witnesses… Charles stopped in mid-thought. Of course. There had been a witness: Buddy Marks. And he had chosen to protect Ames's killer. Why had Buddy done that? Who would he risk his own neck for? He hardly knew Gonzalez-Rivera. That left Paul Turner and Johnny. And Turner and Marks had been best friends. Yes. Turner was the only man Buddy would lie to cover up for. The only one. And Turner might be a no-good rat in many ways, but he would never kill Buddy Marks. Not even to save his own neck. Or would he?

Charles decided to formalize his investigation. He would spend the day systematically questioning all the men he could find before they moved out. He didn't expect to get much from them, but at the very least, his report would show Coleman that he had done his duty to the utmost, and he hoped that perhaps a picture would emerge. Which one of the three suspects was most likely to have raped the German girl? His money was on Turner.

Charles dragged a table and two unstable chairs into an empty room in the old tavern and set up his "office." Next, he had Montana round up the men and bring them upstairs one by one.

Only he and Coleman knew that they were looking for an officer, and that the list of suspects had been narrowed to three, so Donnelly had to tread carefully, drawing the men out with innocuous queries about everything and anything but the murders. By and large the men took it well—respectfully uncom-municative, but with the usual enlisted man's defense of feigned stupidity. But as the long hours of questioning wore on, a definite theme began to emerge, rarely from what any one man said, but more from the way eyebrows raised and fleeting frowns crossed otherwise tight-lipped faces.

Lieutenant Louis Coleman Ames was hated, not only by Turner, but by virtually everyone who knew him. By all accounts, he was an arrogant, dishonorable, stupid bullying coward—probably kicked puppies and hated the Chicago Cubs too, the prick.

Charles wondered how he would couch all this bile in his report. He could just imagine telling Coleman that there was no chance of finding his nephew's killer, because everyone despised him with equal venom.

Moreover, to Donnelly's surprise, Turner seemed to be one of the most popular officers in the regiment. And, while Gonzalez-Rivera was considered shifty, the men seemed to feel safe under his command. St. John, of course, was universally liked, trusted and admired. None of the officers seemed a likely rapist. Nothing was falling into place, and Charles ran his hands over his face in exhaustion and frustration.

Dismissing the last of the men, Charles settled back in his chair and took a much-needed belt of whisky as he considered what he had learned during the course of the day. Now a different light shone on the murder scene. He had heard it said that the considered collective judgment of a village about one of its own is rarely if ever wrong. And in that respect, armies were very much like villages; long proximity under the worst kinds of stress tended to expose a man's true colors.

The fact that everyone hated Ames stuck in Donnelly's gullet. With all he had heard and inferred today, was it really credible to persist in thinking Ames had been the hero that day? And if he wasn't the hero, what was he? Every single man who knew about the rape took it for granted that Ames was the rapist, and whoever shot him had caught him in the act. Could that be true? It certainly made sense to Charles. Then, again, why didn't the officer stop him, arrest him, and make sure he hanged? Charles was becoming more confused than enlightened. One step forward, two back. At this rate, the war would end before he caught Ames's killer.

Just then, Montana walked in, triumphantly holding up a long strip of evil-looking meat.

Charles grimaced. "What on earth is that?"

"Hell, sir, don't you recognize a fine piece of cow's liver when you see it? This here is the best eating in town."

Charles looked unconvinced.

"It's from a cow we liberated over to the southwest meadow. I thought you'd appreciate a special hunk of the animal."

"That's awfully good of you, Montana, but really, you should keep it for yourself."

"Aw, there's enough for everybody. I'll cook it up right now with some onions. There's a wood stove downstairs. You'll like to die it'll taste so good."

Montana was right. Before long, he and Donnelly sat at the table in Charles's office eating a surprisingly tasty mess of liver and wild spring onions. By candlelight, no less.

"So what's this all about sir," Montana asked through a mouthful of food. "That is, if you don't mind my asking."

Charles took a swig from his canteen. "Let me ask you something, Montana. What have you heard about Lou Ames's death?"

"Well, you know, just stuff. Nothing to set no store by, I guess."

"Such as?"

"Don't be telling anyone you got this from me, but word is that Ames was raping some poor girl and got hisself shot by Marks. Ain't that right, sir?"

"Actually, no," Charles said, putting down his empty plate. "It was Ames who walked in on the rape and tried to put a stop to it." By now, Charles didn't believe that, but it was the official theory, and he hoped to draw out Montana as far as he could.

"Begging your pardon, sir, but that don't seem likely to me, no way, no how."

"Oh?"

"Well, a couple of the guys thought they caught Lou Ames raping a girl in Cherbourg right after we come over. He swore she was willing and they was just having a good, healthy screw but he had that big ol' knife he always carried and it'd probably been pointed right at her throat."

"What kind of knife?" Donnelly asked.

"A Bowie, I think. Black leather handle. Lethal looking thing. The girl must have been scared to death. Got the hell out as soon as them other guys showed up. So, I can't see as how he'd much mind if anyone else was doin' the same. Like as not he'd ask for a piece of the action."

"If that's true then why wasn't he brought up on charges? All the girl had to do was report him and he'd have swung just as sure as hell. Not even his uncle could've saved him on that one. You know that."

"Well, sir, it was like I said. We figure she was scared out of her skin. And, besides, it was only enlisted guys what caught him, sir. You think anybody'd believe them over the word of Coleman's nephew? Nah, they kept it to themselves. Besides, the girl might have been willing. We'll never know.

"But to tell the truth, no one was surprised when they heard that he got it. I think the only thing that's got us confused is why you're asking questions about it. Hardly worth the bother. Marks should've got a medal. Which brings me back to my question: What's this all about? You already got your man."

Charles considered his options. By now everyone knew that the investigation was still ongoing, and the killer would be on the alert. He had gotten the information he needed about the officers. There was no more need for secrecy.

"Marks didn't hang himself. He was murdered."

Montana whistled. "So, we still got ourselves a live one."

"Yes, we do. And if I don't find out who it is and fast, I'll probably be joining Ames and Marks." Charles stood up and stretched. "Time to hit the hay. Thanks for the meal and the information, Montana. You've been more helpful than you know."

"Anytime, sir."

Charles listened to Montana's footsteps receding down the tavern stairs. So Ames was the rapist. It made perfect sense. And that meant Charles had been looking at things the wrong way all along. Charles closed his eyes and thought back to his conversation with Johnny. What was it he'd said? "Whoever killed Ames did it because he wanted to… nobody had a reason not to kill Ames." But there was something else. And then he remembered, "Lou didn't even have his gun drawn, for Pete's sake," St. John had said.

His gun. If Lou was the rapist, then Charles had searched the wrong part of the barn for bullets from the killer's gun. Of course there were no shells in the haystacks where the girl had been raped and killed, nor stray bullets in the walls near the entrance. Lou had never gotten off a shot. Whoever shot Ames had been standing in the doorway. If a bullet had missed, it would have lodged in the wood behind the girl's body. It was possible that there was evidence there that he had overlooked. Evidence that could solve this damned case once and for all. He had to get back to that barn.

Charles poked his head into the hallway and listened. A few doors down he could hear Coleman's gruff cough. He was still up. Charles started down the hall to speak to him when he suddenly realized what he was doing. What was he thinking? How could he possibly barge into Coleman's office and tell him his beloved nephew was a vicious rapist? Montana was right. Unless he had absolute proof, he couldn't say a thing.

But then, how could he get permission to go back to the Rhine? Hell, he thought, ask for it.

Charles took a deep breath and knocked on Coleman's door.

"Yes? What is it?" Coleman asked. "Are you all right, Donnelly? You look like you're about to pass out."

"I'm fine, sir," Charles said faintly. "Just exhausted. I'm still getting bad headaches. That shrapnel I took."

"Maybe you need a break. Take some leave. Relax. It'll be a few days before regimental headquarters moves forward."

"Perhaps you're right, sir."

"That's settled then."

"I want to go back to the barn," Charles said. "You've turned me into a real detective."

"Why the barn? Oh, clues, I suppose. Well, good luck, Charles. You could have gone to Paris, you know."

Charles's Jeep crunched to a halt on the dirt track that led downhill to the river's edge. He climbed out of the driver's seat to get his bearings. The landscape seemed familiar, and yet, devoid of soldiers and vehicles, it was a different place, a sylvan landscape of pastures and woodland. Only the dead hulks of the four knocked-out panzers and the foundations of the burnt-out farmhouse, rising like a black crown on the hillside above him, convinced Charles that this was, indeed, the place. Already in the past few days, delicate green leaves had sprouted on the trees, and new grass blanketed the fields. Wild lingonberry bushes lined the road. In a few months they would be heavy with fruit. In front of him, the Rhine drifted by. What had seemed so gray and ominous on the morning of the crossing was now a beautiful ribbon of blue-grey water, nothing more.

Charles walked to the site where the aid station had stood and looked around. There, leading into the woods, was the path. He looked to see if anyone was watching him. Then, certain that no one was, he plunged into the woods.

Moments later, Donnelly stood in the open doorway to the barn. To his untrained eyes, it looked as though no one had been there since his last fruitless visit. Everything was exactly as it had been; even the bloodstained hay had not been disturbed. Charles stepped just inside. This is where the killer would have made his move, he thought. He scanned the ground by his feet looking for shells that he might have missed, but found nothing. Evidently, Ames's killer had cleaned up his trail. "Ames's killer," thought Charles. He had suddenly realized he didn't give a damn who killed Ames. It was the girl he cared about. He was certain Ames slit her throat, but to prove it, he had to find the man who caught Ames and shot him. That narrowed the field. Turner would have, Johnny, too. Marks certainly. Yes. It had to be Marks, but Marks had been murdered, too. Hanged by person or persons unknown.

Charles walked to the back of the barn, hoping for something, anything, that might shed some light. Those .45s were notoriously inaccurate. Just maybe the killer had to fire more than once.

But after an hour of tedious searching, Charles hadn't found anything that could be considered a clue. No remnants of a crime, no stray bullets or strands of hair.

Then, just as he was about to give up, something caught his eye. A glint in the back corner of the barn. Donnelly held his breath and moved closer. There, lodged in a thick wooden support beam, was a small gleam of metal. Closer still, he saw what it was. A bullet.

Very carefully, using a penknife, Charles pried the cartridge out of the wall and wrapped it in his handkerchief. It was a .45, but he could see, to his relief, that the grooves left by the pistol's rifling were intact up to the point the bullet flattened out. Suddenly Charles froze. He could hear heavy footsteps moving towards the barn door. Someone was outside. He drew his .45 and crept into the dark shadows.

"Who's there?" Charles called out loudly.

There was no answer. Instead, the footsteps seemed to recede. Hugging the wall, he moved cautiously to the door and listened. He could hear the footsteps disappearing into the forest.

Charles dashed out of the barn chasing after the intruder. Up ahead he saw a flash of movement. Charles leapt forward into the thicket and came face to face with an old brown cow, quietly munching on a bit of moss. It looked up at Charles quizzically, before moving on in search of better pasture.

Laughing in relief, Charles leaned against a tree and slid to the ground. He patted his pocket to make sure the bullet was still there. Satisfied, he lay down on a bed of old leaves and looked up at the patch of open sky above the treetops. The ground was still wet from last night's rain, but Charles ignored it, yawning and stretching. As he did, his fingertips brushed against something hard and cold. He turned to see what it could be. There, partially buried under the soil in the underbrush a shiny speck of blade winked at him, evidently exposed after the rain had washed away the dirt around it. Charles dug into the ground and lifted out a knife. A Bowie knife, one with a black leather handle. Decayed leaves and what looked like dried blood matted the blade.

Charles shuddered. He knew exactly who the knife had belonged to. But why was it buried here, a good hundred yards from the barn?

8

Donnelly was in no hurry to report to Coleman with the truth about Ames and was tempted to go on to Paris as Coleman had suggested. Three lazy days—wandering through Montmartre, eating respectable food and watching the girls stroll by—was exactly what he needed. But he knew that he had to get back to the regiment. It was time to catch the killer. His commanding officer had given him an assignment, and he had to complete that assignment. Charles couldn't allow his personal feelings about Ames to hinder what he knew his duty to be. He smiled at himself. That was all nothing but rationalization. It was Marks's murder that was unpardonable—and the girl's. Those were Charles's incentives to solve the crime.

✪

Headquarters buzzed with the news that Marks had been murdered. Obviously Montana had lost no time spreading the word after Charles had left. And if everyone knew about Marks, Charles reasoned, they would also know that an officer was suspected of both murders. His questioning sessions had made that abundantly clear. Once again, Charles reminded himself that he would have to watch his step. It was not Ames's murder that sent a chill down his spine. For if Ames had raped the girl, and the evidence of the bullets made it clear that he had, then surely he had slit her throat, though it puzzled Charles that he had found the knife outside.

No, it was the cold-blooded, premeditated murder of Buddy Marks that quickened his pulse and shortened his breath. The man who had done that was someone for whom Buddy had risked his own neck, someone Buddy cared about. Though he couldn't prove it yet, Charles felt that man was Paul Turner. And now, possibly, he had the evidence to prove it.

St. John stood waiting outside the headquarters building as an enlisted man changed a tire on his Jeep. He gave Charles a lazy, laconic greeting. "The word's out you got a leave to Paris. Mighty fast trip to Paris, old man. How were Les Girls?"

"Couldn't tell you. I was more interested in Les Food, I'm afraid," Charles lied.

St. John laughed. "Puritanical old glutton." The man finished replacing the tire and Johnny gave it a kick. "Seems okay. Well, I'm off. See you this evening? And then I want to hear what you really did." He smiled mischievously. But it seemed to Charles that he detected a slight challenge in St. John's voice. Was it possible that he knew where Charles had been?

Upstairs in the tavern, Coleman was in close consultation with a colonel named Trimble. The two bent over the desk, studying a large-scale map of the Main River region.

"Charles. Back so soon?"

"Uh, sir? Can I speak to you for a moment?"

Coleman caught the strain in Donnelly's voice and looked up sharply.

"Well?"

"I went back to the Rhine."

"And what did you find out?"

Charles glanced uneasily at Trimble.

"Come on, come on," barked Coleman good-naturedly. "We haven't time for niceties. Trimble knows about the investigation."

"Yes, a terrible business," said Trimble.

"Sir, I really think..."

"Out with it, man! Don't shilly-shally."

Charles knew he couldn't tell the colonel the truth—that his nephew had raped a young, defenseless German girl. Especially not with Colonel Trimble standing there. He had to think fast. "Sir, I've been studying the murder of your nephew, Lou Ames, and one thing strikes me. It looks to me as if he was standing by the door to the barn when he was shot. The bullet knocked him onto his back, but he was almost certainly facing outward."

Both Coleman and Trimble nodded.

Donnelly hesitated. "So, it's difficult to know exactly what happened. But, Lieutenant Ames must have seen the girl and was on his way out of the barn when someone came in." Charles knew he was being vague and inconclusive, but what were the alternatives?

Coleman nodded, but still seemed puzzled. "So you think the rapist came back? Why would he do that?"

"I don't know, sir. As you can see, I'm still reconstructing the events."

"I see. Well, get to it, man. We need answers."

"Sir, there is one more thing. I think I found the murder weapon. At least the weapon that killed the girl."

Trimble looked excited. "You mean the knife?"

Donnelly looked at Coleman uneasily. "Yes, sir." From his pocket, he withdrew the knife, still encrusted with dried blood. Would Coleman know that it belonged to his nephew? Would he recognize the black leather handle?

Both Coleman and Trimble took in deep breaths.

"That would explain the reason the murderer returned to the barn, sir. He left to dispose of the knife. I found it about a hundred yards from the barn."

"Then why didn't he keep going?" asked Trimble.

Donnelly shrugged. "Maybe he wanted to make sure Ames and the girl were really dead.

"Besides that," Charles continued, "I did another search around the barn for shell casings or spent bullets, anything that could help us."

"Shame you didn't find any," said Trimble. "These days they can do all sorts of clever identification stuff with a bullet. These forensic science fellows could tell you what gun a bullet came from in half a moment."

"Yes, that'd be the thing," agreed Coleman distractedly.

"But I do have a bullet. That's what I came to tell you, sir." Charles delved into his pockets and pulled out the white handkerchief in which he had wrapped the slug.

The effect on Coleman was electric. "Good God, man," he shouted, "why didn't you say so before?"

"You see, we'd all been looking at the front of the barn for stray bullets. If Lou was on his way out, the place to look would be at the back of the barn."

Coleman peered down at the spent bullet. "Still," he said, "does any of this evidence bring us closer to knowing who killed Lou? Or Marks?"

"No sir, I'm afraid not." And, to himself, Donnelly conceded that his new knowledge that Ames was the rapist did not narrow the list of suspects.

"Sir, I'd like your authority to conduct ballistics tests."

Coleman hesitated.

Trimble interrupted, "You know about this bullet testing business, do you?"

"Yes, sir, at least, I've read enough to have a vague idea."

"I understand General Marks is anxious to have his son's killer flushed out. He'll be very pleased to hear that you've found this bullet. Eh, Coleman?"

"He will, indeed. All right, Donnelly, you'd better get cracking on those tests." Coleman returned his attention to the map, indicating the subject was, for now, closed. Donnelly quietly left the room, relieved to get away.

Outside, the village streets were emptying as men headed south toward the line. Charles turned down an unpaved road lined with houses where the officers had been quartered. As he rounded the corner, a bullet ricocheted off the side of a building hitting a wall about two inches above his head. Charles spun around just as Paul Turner appeared, smiling smugly.

"Sniper almost got you, huh, Charlie?"

"What the hell was—"

"We got the bastard," Turner interrupted. "You sure were lucky, though. Close call." He walked off, grinning.

Charles narrowed his eyes as he watched him go. He knew Turner was just trying to scare him. There were no snipers in this village and both men knew it.

The next morning in an old tool shed on the edge of the German village where Coleman's headquarters was still ensconced, Donnelly set up a makeshift ballistics lab. He had sent Montana out to scrounge up a topless, empty oil drum, which he rolled into the shed, then got some men to help him fill it with water, using five-gallon Jerry cans filled from the town pump.

"Montana," he said distractedly, "see if you can get your hands on some envelopes. The company clerk should have some."

With the tank nearly full of water, Charles looked around the tiny space. Everything was ready. It was time to round up his suspects.

✪

St. John sat pensively on a bench in the main square, basking in the warm evening breeze.

"Long day?" asked Charles from behind.

St. John turned. "Long, but productive, I suppose. How are you, Charles?"

"Been better. Look, Johnny, I'm going to need you a little later. You aren't going anywhere are you?"

"No. What's up?"

Charles told St. John about the planned ballistics tests.

"Sounds interesting. How can I help?"

"Well, actually," Charles said, "I need you to shoot your .45."

"What on earth for?"

"I'm afraid that, strictly speaking, you're a suspect. We all are."

"Me? A double murderer? Oh Lord, Charles, you really are the limit. What will my dear old grey-haired mother say?" St. John laughed but to Donnelly, the laughter sounded forced.

"Your mother is dead, Johnny. I hate this business; I know you had nothing to do with it, but the fact is, your movements can't be accounted for. Neither can mine. And whether we like it or not, that makes us all suspects in the colonel's book. I'm sorry."

"Okay. I want to know who killed the girl and Marks just as much as you do. So let's get on with the show."

"Gonzalez-Rivera and Turner are having their guns tested as well."

"Fine with me," said St. John. "Sounds like you expect me to argue with you about this bullet testing. Far from it. Anything to get us forwarder, I say."

Charles found Major Gonzalez-Rivera in his room, lounging on his bed examining a picture of Veronica Lake in a dog-eared copy of *YANK*. He greeted Charles and continued to read the magazine, affecting great interest in the stale news it contained.

Sitting down at Gonzalez-Rivera's table, Charles explained the need for the test. Of course, Gonzalez-Rivera knew already. The man had one ear permanently to the ground, it seemed.

"Fine with me, detective," he said, "I understand entirely."

Charles stood up and spoke with as much authority as he could muster. "I'll expect you there in one hour."

"I'll be there," replied Gonzalez-Rivera casually.

Turner, as Charles had expected, was reluctant to cooperate. He turned him down with a fluency of obscene language that Charles had seldom heard before, despite his three years in the army. Then, he must have remembered something. He smiled and said, "Okay, Sherlock. I'll be there. I was just griping out of habit, I guess."

An hour later, the three officers appeared at the door of the shed where Charles and Coleman waited.

"Inside," Coleman ordered tersely, "and do exactly as Donnelly asks. I'll be in my office if anybody gives you any lip, Lieutenant."

"Wait a minute," Turner said. "With all due respect, sir, why should I have my gun tested while you and Sherlock, here, don't. You carried .45s at the Rhine just like me."

There was a murmur of agreement from Gonzalez-Rivera.

"Very well, Turner," replied Charles, "we'll all have our guns tested, me and Colonel Coleman included. That's equitable, isn't it?"

"That's fair enough," said St. John to Turner. "If the colonel is willing to do it, there's no reason why any of us should mind."

"We will all shoot our pistols," snapped Coleman.

Turner nodded sullenly.

Inside, the five men gathered about the old oil drum in the dank room, shafts of orange light from the setting sun casting lines across their tense faces. To set an example, Charles went first. A loud bang reverberated through the room as he fired into the open top of the oil barrel, followed by a splash of water. Coleman was next, then Turner, St. John and Gonzalez-Rivera. Five bullets fired; five splashes of water.

After each shot, Charles retrieved the bullet from the barrel of water and, being careful not to let any of the others see, placed them in separate envelopes, labeled randomly: A, B, C, D, and E. On a slip of paper he noted the names of each man and the letter corresponding to their sample bullet: A for Donnelly, B for Coleman, C for Gonzalez-Rivera, D for Turner, and E for St. John. He hid the paper away in his wallet. Now no one would be able to claim that the lab tests were tainted by knowledge of the bullet's provenance.

"Happy now, Sherlock?" said Turner as they left the tool shed, emerging into the crisp evening air.

"Happy? No, I wouldn't say that," replied Donnelly. "I don't take any pleasure in this, Captain Turner. But I want to nail Buddy Marks's killer, that's all."

Turner looked pensive, as if he were puzzling something out. Then he walked away.

"Something wrong?" asked Coleman.

"No, sir. Nothing at all."

"Good. So, tell me Charles, what do you do with those bullets now?"

"I get them to C.I.D. They'll send them to a forensic lab in London that's equipped with a comparison microscope. It'll match one of these bullets to the slug I found."

"You'll need to deliver them personally. Make sure you get them to the officer in charge—no one else."

"Yes, sir."

"Regimental headquarters is moving out tomorrow night. We've taken over the sector and driven the Germans all the way back to the Main. Our line companies are just waiting for their supporting units to arrive before assaulting the Germans on the other side. When we move, I'm going to need you with me. How quickly can you do this?"

"Get to C.I.D. and back? If I leave in the morning I can be back by early tomorrow afternoon."

"See that you are."

"Sir, I'd like to leave the bullets in the safe in your office tonight, if it's okay with you. It'll help me sleep better."

"Good idea."

With the envelopes secured in the portable field strongbox in Coleman's office, Charles went in search of St. John but couldn't find him.

On his way back to his room, Charles passed Gonzalez-Rivera on the street outside his billet and waved, but the major looked away, pretending not to have seen Charles, and disappeared around the corner. The day's events had made Charles an outsider, perhaps even an outcast.

The minute Charles entered his room, he knew someone had just been there. He lit a candle and looked around. As he did so it suddenly hit him: the blackout curtains were drawn. He had left the lights out and the windows open. Somebody had been here. Looking for the bullets, no doubt. Charles dragged a chair over to the door and shoved it under the handle. Whoever had been here earlier might come back, and he wasn't taking any chances.

Wearily, Charles began to undress but was interrupted by a knock on his door. "Yes?" he called out suspiciously.

The knock came again, harder this time. "Open up, Donnelly, I don't have all night!" It was Coleman.

Hastily Charles moved the chair and opened the door. "Sorry, sir. Please come in."

"No time for that. Look, the plans have changed. I've just gotten orders that we have to move out tomorrow morning. I need you for a rather tricky mission."

"What about the bullets, sir?"

"You can send them in."

"I'd rather not, sir."

"Then they'll have to wait 'til we get across the Main. No one will touch them in the safe. Charles, I'll need all the officers I have in these next few days. I'm not happy about it but we'll have to bring the killer to justice later. Anyway, I'll feel safer with you away from the rest of the regiment for the next few days. Better than getting a bullet in your back on the battlefield."

"What are my orders?"

"Division's all set to cross the Main tomorrow, but we've got a little pocket of Jerries about twenty miles upriver that we haven't been able to do anything about. It's a crack SS unit. Tough bastards from the Russian front, and we don't want them taking us in the rear after our assault begins."

Charles nodded.

"We've got to push them across to the east bank of the river and keep them there until our main force crosses at Wurzburg, then infantry can march north from there and wipe the bastards out."

"So I'm going to push them across the river?"

"No. First Battalion will handle that just before they move downriver for the main attack."

"And what happens when the First Battalion moves downriver? As soon as the Germans see our men pull out they'll come swarming back. Who's going to keep them on their own side until our infantry arrives?"

"I'll be sending you in as soon as the First Battalion's cleared the town. The river splits the town in two. You'll lead a small force into the town on the west bank of the river opposite the German unit and plant yourselves there just to make sure the enemy doesn't return across the river and raise hell in our rear."

"What sort of a unit are you sending me in with?"

"I'm giving you a gun from your old outfit, the Antitank Company, plus a light machine gun squad from Easy Company. I'm also giving you a squad of riflemen and a medic. You'll have a radio, so you can let me know if you get into any trouble."

"How many men does this SS outfit have?"

"We're not absolutely sure. You know how unreliable our intelligence estimates are." Coleman dug into his pocket. "Charles, you told me about the problems you're having with our suspects. You're dealing with two captains and a major, and you are only a first lieutenant. So, I'm promoting you to the rank of captain, effective immediately. I've brought you these."

Charles took the two sets of double silver bars from the colonel. Donnelly was pleased. "Thank you, sir." It hadn't sunk in that the colonel had changed the subject away from the strength of the SS unit that would be opposing him.

"I know you'll do me proud, Charles." Coleman handed Donnelly a small map. "Let's go over this. I'll show you where you'll pick up your three units."

An hour later, Charles finally flopped into bed, the silver bars glinting in his hand. Where once he would have been apprehensive, even scared, he was now actually looking forward to the coming mission. The murder investigation had been preying on his mind, weighing him down. Anything was better than that. Even combat. He fell into a profound sleep.

9

On a wooded rise above the west bank of the Main River in a stand of pine trees, Donnelly sat in his Jeep, looking down on the small town of Belingen on the Main. Beside him, Montana calmly smoked a cigarette.

Belingen appeared to be a working class factory town with none of the once opulent, but now destroyed, mansions that Donnelly had seen in many other river towns. Dingy apartment buildings lined the narrow streets. The river, where the fighting was taking place, lay hidden from their view by warehouses, offices, and the smoke stacks of small manufacturing plants, but it was easily discernible. Above the water, a cloud of black smoke rose furiously into the sky. Charles could hear the popping of rifles and the chatter of machine guns, punctuated by the explosions of mortar shells.

It was already mid-afternoon, and Charles wanted to go in before dark. He looked at his watch. "This thing should've been finished by now."

"Yes, sir," drawled Montana. He gestured toward the town. "Looks like the First Battalion's coming out. But it don't look to me like the fight's over yet."

Donnelly jumped out of the Jeep and walked to the road for a better view. To his left, about three hundred feet down the road, he saw two columns of American infantry heading toward him. Charles waited until the men of the first few units trudged past his Jeep. He spotted a lieutenant leading his platoon. "What's going on?" demanded Donnelly. "Have you pushed the Krauts across the river already?"

"Pretty much," the lieutenant replied. "A few are still fighting on this side, but we've got orders to move out. They need us for the main assault."

"Damn!" Charles muttered, but he had no time to argue. He needed to get his men into the town and secure his side of the Main River before the Germans discovered the G.I.'s were pulling out and they could retake the town if they took advantage of the situation and launched a full-scale attack.

He went back to the Jeep and called over his three sergeants. The only one he'd known before was Glen Miller of Antitank, a good, reliable soldier. The other two were the rifle squad leader, Terry Kaplan, and the machine gunner, Dennis Grant.

"Okay," Donnelly said quickly. "Here's the plan: We leave the vehicles here. There's only one road going into town so we'll have to share it with the First Battalion troops leaving. But we'll still move in, spread out in two columns. When we get to town, there are three main streets to the river. Kaplan, your squad will take the one in the center. Miller, go right. Grant, left. There shouldn't be any resistance, but if there is, clean it out and we'll join forces at the riverfront. Any questions?"

"Captain," asked Miller, "isn't First Battalion supposed to chase all the Krauts out before we go in?"

Donnelly nodded. "That's the plan. But it looks to me like the battalion's pulling out already, and I want to be in position before they leave so we can take on any Krauts who might want to cross back to our side of the river."

"Then, sir, I suggest we get going," said Kaplan.

"Right," Donnelly agreed. "I'll lead the column and stay with Kaplan's men to the river. Go form your squads and prepare to move out. The trucks and Miller's gun will come in after dark. Montana will mount guard on them."

The two files of infantrymen slogged down the road, heavily laden with bandoleers of ammunition, hand grenades and rifles;

the pockets of their field jackets bulged with K rations; some carried parts of a .30 caliber light machine gun; almost every man carried a case of machine gun ammunition for the one gun the small unit possessed. Most carried their bedrolls over their shoulders. They didn't trust their trucks to make it into town. Periodically, a man's rifle would hit his steel helmet with a dull clunk. They could have been any American combat infantry unit in Europe that spring of 1945.

Filing past them in the opposite direction, the men of the First Battalion lumbered out of the town. In contrast to Donnelly's soldiers, they looked worn and weary. Occasionally one of the G.I.'s called out a greeting or a wisecrack to one of the men headed in the opposite direction, but neither group was relaxed. Both were going into battle, the First Battalion into the main assault; Donnelly's men into the town—three squads relieving an entire battalion—twenty-nine men replacing eight hundred.

To Donnelly's relief, the shooting in Belingen had diminished to sporadic volleys of rifle fire and infrequent mortar explosions. Did this mean that the Germans had finally been pushed across the river? Donnelly wondered. So now were both sides simply making their presence known? He certainly hoped so. First Battalion men streamed out of every street in organized units, as planned. It would not be necessary to fight their way in.

Donnelly stopped and raised his hand to halt the columns. Instantly, Kaplan appeared at his side.

"Have your squad close up a bit, sergeant. The town's secure. Continue in two columns and follow me."

As an officer came abreast from the opposite direction, Donnelly asked, "Where's your battalion C.P.?"

The man turned and pointed down the street toward the river. Donnelly followed his directions to a large building where several G.I.'s were removing the sign, which read HEADQUARTERS—FIRST BATTALION. Halting his columns again, Charles entered the building, leaving Kaplan in charge of the men.

The captain inside, an older man with a slight stubble of a beard, looked at Donnelly hopefully. "You're Donnelly from Coleman's regiment, come to take over. Am I right?"

Charles nodded.

"Excellent. Your timing couldn't be better. We're pulling out. Just finished chasing the last Germans across the river. All you have to do is keep them there. Good luck." With that he started out the door.

"Hang on a second," Donnelly shouted. "I need to be briefed. Show me your map. Tell me the situation."

The few remaining men were leaving the battalion C.P. hurriedly, brushing past Donnelly and the other captain.

"Look, Captain, I just finished telling you. The Krauts are on the other side of the river. Keep them there. That's all."

"How many men?" asked Charles. "What're their strong points?"

"Don't know," replied the captain. "We just chased the bastards out of here. God knows where the rats have holed up now. All I know is we got orders to move our ass down river immediately, if not sooner, and that's what we're doing."

"How many Krauts?" shouted Donnelly at the disappearing back of the captain.

Without stopping, he turned and yelled back, "Five, six hundred, maybe."

"What?" Charles practically screamed. "Five or six hundred?"

"Just don't let them get onto the bridge," he heard the captain say before disappearing from sight.

Bridge, thought Charles. Nobody mentioned any bridge. He thought the Germans always blew their bridges behind them. But not these tough apples. They meant to come back across.

Charles felt himself breaking out in a clammy sweat. What the hell was going on?

A moment later, Charles stood alone in the command post. The First Battalion was gone; he was in command of three under-strength squads whose mission was to keep a horde of fanatical

Nazi troops from crossing the Main and attacking American units downriver. But the plain fact was, he didn't have enough soldiers to do the job. He'd be lucky if he and his men survived an hour, once the shooting started. Charles was an obsessive worrier. In his mind, he knew he was staring at failure. A crucial failure. One that could result in the deaths of thousands of men and the defeat of an American army. A failure that would result in his own court-martial and probable death by firing squad—that is, of course, unless the Germans got him in the next few hours.

Leaving the Command Post, he hurried down to the river's edge to reconnoiter the waterfront. His sergeants followed him, leading their columns of men.

The river got narrower here with a slower current. And there was a bridge, all right—a steel and concrete span that the Germans must have used to cross the river just ahead of the First Battalion riflemen, who hadn't followed because they were under orders not to. The bridge was damaged but usable. Anytime now the enemy might come pouring back across it.

Charles shook his head and sighed. How the hell had they gotten into this predicament? Then, suppressing his deep sense of foreboding, he turned to his sergeants, who were standing nearby awaiting his command. "Grant! Miller! Kaplan!"

Grant approached quickly. "What are my orders, sir?"

"I need your machine gun positioned so its fire will stop anybody trying to come across that bridge. And hurry—we don't have much time. As soon as they realize that most of the troops have pulled out, they're sure to attempt a crossing." Grant disappeared before Donnelly finished his last sentence.

Miller stepped forward. "Sir, where do you want my men?"

Charles thought quickly. The antitank gun was still on the hill outside of town, attached to its truck. Upriver, Charles had spotted an abandoned warehouse. From there the antitank gun could cover the river itself, in case the SS decided to cross in boats.

"We'll bring the 57 into town after dark and put it in that warehouse," said Donnelly, pointing to the building. "Go check it out, Glen."

"Yes, sir," confirmed Miller as he trotted off with his gun squad.

Terry Kaplan stood next to Donnelly, listening and sizing things up. "I believe you'll want me to place my riflemen in other buildings along the waterfront to cover the 57 and Grant's machine gun, won't you, sir?"

"You got it," Donnelly answered appreciatively. He liked this young sergeant.

The building that had served as the battalion headquarters made a perfect C.P. for Donnelly. Half a block back from the Main, it was far enough away from the river not to be under direct fire from the enemy, yet close enough to allow Charles to get to the riverfront quickly. He put the men on guard in shifts of two hours, so half his force would be at the river at all times and the other half would be readily available if necessary. He had instructed the men to sleep in the C.P. during their off-hours.

When all the preparations were made, Charles slipped into an empty room in the C.P. and stood alone, looking out at the darkening sky. He rubbed his hands together for warmth. Already, the air had turned chilly and damp and nighttime would drop the temperature even more. He replaced the blanket used for a black-out curtain and reached into his pocket for a candle and some matches. As he lit it, he heard a footstep on the flagstone floor.

"Sir, it's dark now." It was Kaplan. "Don't you think we should bring in the antitank gun?"

"Yes. Send the two drivers. With Montana, they can bring in everything: the gun, the other truck and my Jeep. Tell them, 'No lights.'"

Kaplan saluted in the shadows of the candlelit room and left.

Nice kid, Donnelly thought, as he watched him go. Intelligent, too. But young… too young to face what they were up against.

Donnelly joined the off-duty riflemen in the larger outer room of the C.P. Some sat, some stood and jabbered nervously; all of them were tense, waiting for something to happen.

Charles tried his best to relax. But every time he did that, he began to think of the damned murder Coleman had assigned him to solve. No, dammit, he thought, three murders. At least, he knew Ames had killed the girl. But who killed Ames and Buddy? He presumed the same man murdered them both. But could he assume that? He shrugged. He reviewed the suspects: Turner, Gonzalez-Rivera, Johnny, even Coleman and me, he thought... No. I don't think—

A sudden series of explosions split the silence of the night. Donnelly threw himself onto the hard stone floor, landing alongside one of the riflemen. They waited there a long moment, eyeball to eyeball, but there were no more explosions. Donnelly quickly got to his feet and brushed himself off. Seconds later Sergeant Grant came through the door, followed closely by Sergeant Kaplan.

"The Jerries threw in three mortar shells down by the bridge," Grant said, his voice flat and toneless. "They must've heard us 'arm' the machine gun."

"If they heard that, what will they do when they hear the trucks rumble in?" Charles asked anxiously.

"They'll plaster us good," Grant said matter-of-factly.

Kaplan interrupted, "I suggested to Sergeant Miller that he meet the vehicles on the outskirts of town and then park them under cover next to the far buildings. After they drop the truck, Miller and his crew can wheel the gun to the river without making any noise."

Donnelly nodded, his relief apparent. "Good thinking, Sergeant."

"You know, sir," continued Kaplan, "we really ought to destroy that damned bridge."

Donnelly smiled in spite of himself. "Yes, sergeant, I know. But we don't have enough explosives to do the job."

"Yes, sir, but I wondered if we could get the artillery to put a few shells onto it? Are they close enough, do you think?"

"I don't know," answered Donnelly, thoughtfully. "But there's one way to find out." He turned to the radioman. "See if you can get regiment for me."

"You want the colonel?" asked the man.

"No," said Charles slowly. "He'll be busy as hell. Get me Captain St. John and tell him I need him bad."

It was nine o'clock. Except for the three mortar shells that had fallen by the bridge, it had remained eerily quiet. As darkness fell, Charles hoped the Germans on the other side of the river would be content to stay there and merely keep his soldiers from crossing. If he could just hold them at bay until the American forces crossing downriver arrived to clean them out...

But the sound of the light machine gun's measured popping shattered his optimism. From his reputation, Charles knew Dennis Grant wouldn't shoot at shadows. Donnelly was out the door and on his way to the river in seconds. He ducked into the store where he'd positioned the light .30 caliber machine gun to fire out an open window. The gun stood silent now.

"What's up?" he called into the darkness.

Sergeant Grant rose from the floor where the gun sat on its tripod. "The Krauts got a patrol across the river. They must've swum. Nobody heard them or saw them. We caught the bastards leaving. Slithering into the water like a nest of eels. We got a couple, but it don't make no difference. We didn't get 'em all, and the ones who got back will tell their buddies what we got here, which, as you and me both know, Captain, ain't much."

Donnelly nodded. The enemy would soon come swarming across. "Okay, Sergeant, keep a good lookout," he said. "Don't let them come over the bridge." He turned to Montana who had appeared beside him. "Alert the riflemen on guard and tell Miller to be sure his gun covers the river. I think some of the Nazis will try to come in boats. Miller can blast them out of the water."

Donnelly left the building and ran back to the C.P.

"Everybody up. Everybody up."

The men jumped to their feet, pulled on their boots, checked their guns and ammo and were ready for action in seconds.

"Okay, men," yelled Donnelly. "You all know where your posts are. Get there on the double. The Germans are going to try to come across."

Donnelly raced for the empty warehouse where he'd placed Kaplan with half of his rifle squad. He knew that Miller and Grant were experienced and competent. But Kaplan was an unknown, just a kid who could probably use Donnelly's help.

Donnelly reached the warehouse just as the first confirmation of the enemy's intentions came with the exploding mortar shells along the American side of the riverfront. Every building was struck. Kaplan's men lay on the floor covering their helmets with their hands, and miraculously nobody got hit. The instant the explosions stopped, the men rose to take their positions again. But, already, German troops raced across the bridge. Others scurried along the riverbank on the American side. How had they crossed? The firing of the light .30 and M-1 rifles told Donnelly his men were fighting back. He heard the 57 fire several times. The battle raged. He'd done his best—now everything lay in the hands of the fighting men. But what the hell had gone wrong? How could he be left here on the west bank of the Main with so few soldiers to fight this futile battle?

Donnelly fired his .45 at the dark forms of enemy soldiers as they appeared outside, running past the long, low windows of the warehouse.

Instinct told him to get out of the building. The Germans would start throwing hand grenades through those windows any second.

"Out. Everybody out," yelled Kaplan before Donnelly had a chance to open his mouth.

"Come on. Come on." shouted Donnelly.

They came out shooting. The Germans now swarmed over the American side of the river. Donnelly glanced up at the bridge. It was littered with bodies. At least the machine gun was preventing any Germans from getting across it. In the brief time he had to look, Charles couldn't spot any landing craft. Yet the Germans were everywhere. Where in hell were they coming from?

Charles unhooked a hand grenade from his belt, pulled the pin, held the grenade, counted silently, then tossed it into the river. Its explosion was muffled, but the shrieks of the Germans in the water were not. Now Donnelly knew. The Krauts were swimming across the river. Those being shot off the bridge were decoys. The whole damned SS was coming at them.

Kaplan's riflemen didn't need to be told. Already they were throwing grenades into the water, as they'd seen the captain do. Now the enemy soldiers turned back for the far shore, swimming for their lives. Those who had made it over were picked off by Kaplan's riflemen.

Bodies washed up on the riverbanks; the wounded groaned amid the carnage; but the firing went on unabated. Suddenly, German mortar shells began falling on the American side of the Main, tearing it to pieces. Charles hit the ground hard as mortars exploded all around him. He felt his leg jerk up as something stung his heel.

"How can they mortar us like this?" Kaplan screamed above the firing. "Their own men are still over here! Their wounded are here!"

"These aren't your normal German soldiers," Charles shouted back. "These scum are an SS unit right off the Russian front. They want this side of the river badly, and they don't care how many of their own men they have to kill to get—" A mortar shell exploded in the building behind him, cutting Donnelly's sentence short.

As a few scattered mortar rounds hit the road, Charles sensed bits of steel whizzing over his body, missing him by fractions of an inch. Thank God the river bank was higher than the road, Charles thought, as he watched the ground exploding above him.

Donnelly knew he should get his men away from the river-front, but if he did, the Germans would wipe them out and take the town. Either way, they were probably going to die tonight.

Artillery. He needed artillery.

The explosions began moving upriver, away from Donnelly towards Glen Miller's gun. Charles looked up and realized that his men had already pulled back from the river. There were no more cries from the German wounded. They had all been killed by their own mortars. Getting painfully to his feet, but still crouching on all fours, Donnelly hobbled painfully back down the street to the open door of the C.P. and bolted inside. He stood there gasping for breath.

"You made it, sir." Kaplan's voice came from the dark. "I was just sending a man to get you."

"I thought I'd got it that time for sure," Donnelly panted. "We have to head back to the river; they'll come across again as soon as they think we've retreated."

"These officers say they have a better idea, sir."

Donnelly strained to see in the dark.

"Hello, Charles," came a familiar voice. "You called, I believe?"

"Johnny!" The words leapt from Donnelly's mouth. "I've never been happier to see anyone in my life."

St. John turned to the officer beside him. "Charles Donnelly, meet Lieutenant Tom Ciccone, artillery forward observer."

"Thank God. Has Kaplan briefed you?"

"He has," Ciccone nodded.

"Can you hit them?" asked Donnelly.

"No problem. I'm with corps artillery. We've got 155 Long Toms."

Donnelly nodded impatiently, knowing Ciccone referred to his long range artillery pieces. "Lieutenant, hurry please. It's now or never."

"You got it." Ciccone spoke into his radio giving the coordinates of the target. Minutes later the scream of a single shell sent Donnelly and his men to the floor. The explosion was deafening.

"Son of a bitch!" shouted Donnelly. "That was on our side of the river!"

"Be patient." Ciccone began to give corrections through the radio. Another whistling, screaming shell. This time it hit in the middle of the river. Donnelly heard the water gush into the air.

A third shell whistled above them like a series of dreadful screams. This time the explosion came from the other side of the river. The shell hit a building with a muffled boom. Donnelly heard walls crashing into the street.

"That's it. That's it. Fire for effect," he yelled to Ciccone. The artillery lieutenant was already giving instructions into the radio before the words were out of Donnelly's mouth.

Shells screamed overhead. This noise could drive a man mad, Donnelly thought.

"Kaplan," Charles shouted. "Let's get back to the river."

"Yes, sir."

As they were leaving, Donnelly shouted to St. John and the forward observer, "Wait here. I'll be back."

"You're very good, Kaplan," Charles said, as the two men hurried back to the river, Charles limping badly. "When'd you come over?"

"End of December. Got drafted in June right after I graduated from high school."

Donnelly shook his head. "High school? How old are you?"

"Turned nineteen in March, sir."

The two men slowed their pace. "You made sergeant pretty fast."

"It was that kind of a winter," said Kaplan. "If you lasted more than a couple of days, you had to replace a sergeant who didn't."

"It's been a rough war."

"Yes, sir."

At the riverbank, the light of burning buildings on the other side of the Main revealed the devastation inflicted by the 155 mm Long Tom cannons. Charles sighed with relief. His men had regained the initiative. Now, with artillery support, they were creaming the SS bastards. By the bridge, Grant's machine gun fired into houses on the opposite bank where the Nazis had taken refuge. Miller's 57 was also firing.

"Save your ammunition," Charles shouted above the din, but the firing did not cease.

"Kaplan," he yelled. "Send a man down to Sergeant Miller. Tell him to save his ammo until he has targets. Tell Grant the same." Kaplan quickly disappeared into the night.

Charles looked toward the river. The moon shone brightly now, the clouds that had concealed it skidding away on the breath of a wind. It occurred to him that the enemy hadn't thrown in a single mortar round since the artillery began firing. He bet the Germans had pulled back from the river, just as he had. In a second, he was running back to the C.P. where he'd left Ciccone and St. John. "Put rounds further into the town. Back from the river. I think that's where the rats have gone."

Moments later, as he limped back to the river, he heard the shrieking of American shells above him, and saw dust rise from far inside the eastern part of Belingen across the river. The bombardment continued for fifteen more minutes.

Then, finally, it stopped. Donnelly stared across the river at the now blazing town. Behind him, he heard Ciccone's voice. "Well, that should give you some relief, Captain. We've got to go now. As it is, I'll probably catch hell for this."

"Why?" asked Charles. "You did a great job."

"Yeah, but we're supposed to be concentrating all our fire on the main objective downriver. As far as the brass is concerned, this little fracas doesn't even exist. Just for being here, I could get my ass in a sling." Ciccone paused. "But, what the hell? I owed Johnny a favor."

"You saved our lives, Ciccone." Charles looked around for St. John. He spotted him close by, sitting on an old concrete wall, and walked over.

"I'm sure you didn't feel the slightest bit afraid during that little exchange of firepower..."

"Of course not, Charles. What's to fear about a few hand grenades flying around?"

Charles smiled. "Nothing, if you're Juggernaut Johnny. Anyway," Charles replied, "thanks."

St. John shrugged. "Don't worry about it. I was hanging around headquarters when your guy radioed in. Figured you could use some company."

"What? You didn't think I could handle five hundred Krauts all by myself?"

St. John grinned. "Sure you could, Charles. But you know I never like to miss a party." He patted Charles on the back. "Kaplan told me the Krauts swam across. That's not like them."

Charles nodded. "It is odd."

"What's over here? There has to be something important. Otherwise they'd have tried to cross someplace else and by-pass you guys."

"As soon as we got here the shooting started. I haven't had time to check out the town."

St. John called out, "Hey, Tommy. Give me a few more minutes. I need to do a bit of scouting."

"Make it fast," came Ciccone's voice from the shadows.

"Come on, Charles, let's do some detective work. You haven't lost your touch just because you're back in the infantry, I hope?" St. John laughed.

As they disappeared into the shadows, Donnelly called back to Kaplan, "You're in charge until I get back."

When they were alone, moving away from the river's edge, St. John whispered, "Charles, what about the ballistics test? Did you get the results?"

"Not yet, Johnny. Coleman sent me here before I had a chance to get the slugs to C.I.D."

Despite Donnelly's swollen foot, Charles and St. John walked swiftly down the darkened streets of Belingen, their eyes alert for anything that might be of particular interest to the SS. Somewhere in this tired, depressed little town was something that the German soldiers were willing to die for. Charles was sure he could feel the eyes of civilians boring into his back from their hiding places in the darkened houses. His ears were alert for the slightest noise. A tug in his heart made him desperate to turn back. But Johnny charged ahead, seemingly fearless as usual.

Rounding a corner, they reached a small town square. On the other side stood a large hospital, covering an entire block. Its heavy front doors were padlocked, but Charles could see a tiny glow of light behind a blackout curtain in an upstairs window, where some careless person had been sloppy when they closed the curtain.

"There're people in there," St. John whispered.

Charles nodded. "Don't think they're tending to our wounded, either."

They crept up to the entrance and tried the padlock. A rusty old thing, it practically fell open in St. John's hand.

"Decoy," St. John said softly. He slowly turned the door handle and, sure enough, the left side of the double door swung inward. They entered quietly and headed up an unlit staircase toward the glimmer of light on the second floor. Upstairs, they stopped on a balcony in front of a pair of swinging doors. Charles could barely make out a long hallway punctuated by many doors. Stretchers and gurneys lined the walls. Beckoning Charles to follow him, St. John made his way down the hall. A slight glow slipped out from beneath the last door on the left. As the men got nearer, they heard faint moans, and the distinct sound of someone swearing softly in German. Donnelly and St. John glanced at each other and, in unison, clicked off the safeties of their pistols. Approaching the door on tiptoe, they pushed it ajar and peered in at a small ward of cots, lit by a single oil lamp. Three men lay in the beds, bandaged and semiconscious—oblivious to the two American soldiers at the door.

St. John nudged Donnelly and pointed at the men's clothes hung on hooks at the bottom of the beds; black tunics and peaked caps grimed with dust, but not so dirty as to obscure the silver insignias gleaming sinisterly in the dim light.

"SS," whispered St. John urgently. "They're goddam SS officers!"

A creak of floorboards made them jump.

A hoarse voice whispered behind them, *"Wass ist los?"*

They spun round. An elderly man in an orderly's uniform stood in the opposite doorway peering at them suspiciously.

"What the hell?" exclaimed Donnelly.

The old man blinked. *"Sheisse! Americanische!?"*

He turned and tried to hobble away, but Donnelly and St. John were on him in a flash.

"Not hurt me. Not hurt me. *Kamerad."* cried the old man.

"Calm down," whispered St. John, setting their captive firmly in a chair. "We won't harm you, *verstehen?"*

St. John questioned the man in fluent German. The man answered him reluctantly, his sentences short and halting. Afterward, Johnny grabbed Donnelly by the arm. "Let's get out of here."

When they were out on the street, Johnny explained what he had learned.

"You have a problem here, Charles. A big problem. Those men are SS generals. Very big pigs. Got hit in a strafing raid by our fighter planes. None of them can walk. Those Nazis across the river were sent here as a security guard for the generals, but our First Battalion took the town too fast for them to get their elite super-pricks out. Now they're under orders from the top to rescue the generals before our Intelligence people can get to them."

"Damn, Johnny, you know what this means? Besides keeping the Jerries on their own side of the river, I've got to keep their generals inside the hospital."

"Right. And you can't let anybody from the hospital cross the river to the enemy side. Okay?"

"I'll do my best," Charles said, as they neared the river.

Ciccone paced anxiously, and looked up in irritation as he saw them approach. "Let's go, Johnny," he urged.

This time St. John was ready. He turned and whispered to Charles as he left. "When I get back, I'm going to explain the situation and try to get you some reinforcements. But don't hold your breath; I'm not optimistic. They're concentrating everything downriver, where the Krauts are still fighting like hell."

"I know," said Charles glumly. "It's only thanks to you we're still here at all. I have a funny feeling Coleman set me up. But why?"

"Don't be an ass, Charles. None of us knew anything about the situation here. It should have been routine—"

"Johnny, come on," shouted Ciccone. "We gotta get out of here."

"I'm on my way." St. John slung a pack over his shoulder and waved good-bye to Donnelly. "See you in a day or two, Charles."

"Wait a minute," cried Donnelly. "What about the bridge? It's still intact. When will your artillery knock out the bridge?" he shouted.

"Sorry, man," Ciccone shouted back. "If I call in one more fire mission on this place, me and all of us here'll get court-martialed."

With that, they were gone.

10

Charles slumped down on a wrought-iron bench inside his command post. Blackout blankets still covered the windows, but the candle was almost burnt out, so he lit another.

As long as the SS generals were on his side of town, the Germans would keep sending men across. He had to get them out of here—had to deliver them safely into the hands of military intelligence. Once they were gone, the bastards across the river would disappear, too.

He reached down and unbuckled his combat boot. His foot throbbed from the mortar slivers, though the wounds were superficial, like burrs in his heel, but if he didn't clean them out, he could get gangrene and lose his foot.

He felt the presence of someone at the door. Donnelly quickly extinguished the candle and peered at the silhouette. "That you, Miller?"

"Yes, sir. Where are you?"

"Over here." Charles hoisted himself to his feet. After the door closed, he re-lit the candle.

"You hit, Captain?" Miller said as he noticed Charles's boot lying on the floor.

"A little shrapnel in my heel. Nothing serious." He was trying hard to sound casual. Actually, he was scared to death he'd get gangrene and lose his foot. "What's been going on in your sector?"

"Well, sir, the Krauts tried to cross in assault boats at my end of town. We sunk five of them, the rest turned back."

"You did well." Charles winced as he tried to put weight on his foot.

"Sir, you need a medic. I can send Corporal Olsen."

"Yes, thanks."

Miller disappeared and returned a few minutes later with the medic. In the meantime, Donnelly had two of his soldiers put more tarps over the windows and light candles and kerosene lamps.

As Olsen cleaned the wound, Charles questioned him about casualties.

"Four men are dead. Nine wounded, besides yourself. Five went back to their posts after I cleaned them up, the other four are hit bad. With your permission, sir, I'd like to bring them back here to the C.P. You have a couple of extra rooms you ain't using."

Donnelly nodded.

"But I'll need more supplies if I'm expected to keep them alive, sir." As he spoke, the medic wrapped a large bandage around Donnelly's foot.

"How the hell can I wear a boot over this thing?"

"We'll cut the heel out, sir."

But after sawing away at the boot for several minutes, it became obvious that this tactic wouldn't work. There wasn't any way Charles could get his foot into a combat boot.

The medic seemed embarrassed that he didn't know exactly what he could do to help his captain. To make conversation while he thought, he said, "Well, sir, one thing I'm glad of; we don't have any of them shell-shock cases. I saw one once. Awful. Guy was froze with fear. Just stared into space, sir. Couldn't move. All he could say was, 'Can't take it no more. Can't take it no more.'"

Charles nodded. "Yeah," he said. "I know. Some men just break down—emotionally, mentally, physically. What amazes me is why every American infantryman in Europe isn't shell-shocked. Damned if I know why, but we aren't."

"Maybe we are," said the medic thoughtfully. "And we just don't know it."

Charles nodded and smiled grimly. "Look, Olsen, there's a hospital a few blocks from here. It looks deserted but I happen to know that it's open for business. They'll have slippers. Get one for my left foot. More importantly, get the supplies and medicine you need and get help from the doctors there. Enough men have died tonight. Take Sergeant Kaplan and a couple of riflemen with you for muscle. I doubt the doctors'll be very cooperative. Tell Kaplan to leave some men there to keep watch tonight. Oh, and I need to talk to him as soon as he gets back. Tell him to come find me right away."

As soon as Olsen left, a weary Charles Donnelly looked around the command post. In the entrance hall, exhausted soldiers slept through the quiet moans of the wounded, who were being brought in and put in a back room. Charles sat down on a blanket on the floor. A second later he was asleep.

His sleep was fitful, constantly disrupted by the throbbing pain in his foot. At one point in the night, he dreamt a beautiful nurse knelt down beside him and swabbed his brow with a damp cloth. Her eyes, gentle and loving, made Charles feel as if he were the only man on earth.

He reached out and caressed her long brown hair. She wasn't a dream. She was real. "You're beautiful," he managed to say. "Who are you?"

"Shhh," she answered. "You must rest."

"I love you," he whispered to her. "I will always love you."

She smiled radiantly then moved to his left foot and unwrapped the bandage. Suddenly the pain vanished and the dream ended.

The tarps on the windows already removed, the dawn crept through and woke Donnelly gently. He smiled, remembering the half dream/half reality and the words he had spoken. Never before had he told a woman he loved her—other than his mother, of course.

He rose and hobbled to the door. He noticed a blue slipper covering his foot. Olsen must have come back and replaced the bandages.

Montana sat in the doorway. Charles sat down next to him.

"Been up long?" Charles asked.

"Maybe. Somebody had to watch over you. You were twitching in your sleep like a frisky bull. Bad dreams?"

"Not so bad," Charles said with a smile.

"Wish you'd saved some for me." Montana laughed. He lit a cigarette and handed it to Charles. "I was just about to have my coffee. Want some, sir?"

"Hot?"

"Yeah. We liberated a blowtorch a while back. It doesn't make any smoke, and it heats things mighty quick."

Charles pulled a breakfast K ration out of his field jacket and tossed it to his driver. "Here's some more coffee, a fruit bar and some ham and eggs. See if you can make me a gourmet breakfast, will you?"

"A silk purse out of a sow's ear, sir?" Montana grinned.

As the two men squatted on the floor with their canteen cups in their hands, Donnelly told Montana about the Nazi officers.

"Boy, oh, boy. Pity Colonel Coleman didn't know what we were in for. He'd have sent a lot more men."

"Captain St. John said he'd try to send help, but I doubt there are any men to spare."

Montana sat up tall. "We can tough it out, sir. We have before."

"Thanks, Montana. Between you and me, I need all the confidence you can spare." Charles stood up and tested his foot. "Better get going. See you later, cowboy."

Charles couldn't help but notice the chilling silence as he made his way to the building by the bridge where Sergeant Grant kept watch.

"Seen any movement, Sergeant?"

"Nothing happening at all, sir. Been dead quiet over there. I think the artillery pounding took all the piss out of them."

"They'll get nasty again as soon as they realize they're not getting shelled anymore.

Grant nodded. "We'll be ready for them, sir. Ready and waiting."

"That's the spirit. Where's Kaplan?"

"Still holed up in the warehouse."

"He was supposed to come find me last night."

"He did. You were out cold, sir. Miller says you got hit. How's the foot?"

"It'll get me where I need to go," Donnelly said, as he set off towards the rifle squad. He hoped that the medic had relayed his orders to leave guards outside the hospital.

Kaplan, like Grant, was watching from a window. He seemed to have all his men with him. Half were asleep and the other half were in positions by the windows.

"Kaplan!"

"Sir!"

"Didn't Olsen give you my message last night?"

"Yes he did, sir. I posted guards outside the hospital, after we'd liberated the stuff Olsen needed."

"Oh, thank God." Donnelly sighed in relief. "And was everything quiet?"

"Nothing to report, sir. I just sent a couple of riflemen down to relieve a few minutes ago."

"Good."

"I didn't see anything much worth protecting in there. Why the guards, Captain?"

"There are a bunch of SS generals in there, waiting to be rescued. The troops across the river are under orders to get them out." Donnelly reached into his pockets and found a crumpled chocolate bar and offered half of it to Kaplan. "I just wish I knew how they plan to do it," he said, thinking aloud.

"Sir," Kaplan said hesitantly, "you know those guys the Jerries sent swimming at us?"

"What about them?"

"I was just thinking, sir. Some of them came over stripped to their underwear. Does that mean anything to you?"

Donnelly caught on to Kaplan's train of thought at once. "It means they came over unarmed. Either they were coming over to surrender, or they have arms and ammunition cached on this side of the river. We know they weren't surrendering. So where are their weapons?"

Kaplan smiled. "I think I know."

Donnelly followed Terry Kaplan's gaze out the long, open window of the warehouse. "My men say that they took out a bunch of Krauts who were trying to lift one of those." Kaplan pointed across the street at a row of large manholes, near the river's edge.

"We need to get down there and check," said Donnelly.

"But if any of us so much as shows himself out there, they'll mortar the hell out of us."

"Maybe not," Donnelly said. "Take a look. Where are they going to observe from?"

On the opposite side of the river, the village of Belingen lay in ruins. Jagged fragments of walls still stood, but the town had been shelled to death. The two- and three-story buildings that had lined the eastern bank of the Main had been reduced to rubble. Yet even as he looked, Donnelly heard the clanking and clinking of metal on metal. Behind the torn walls of the houses that had once been their fortresses, the Germans were setting up mortars. They had recovered from the shelling and were preparing to fight again.

"Cover me," said Donnelly. Without waiting for an acknowledgment, he dashed out the door at the side of the warehouse and ran, limping on his slippered left foot, to the first manhole cover. He grabbed the ring on top of it and pulled. As he struggled to get the heavy lid loose, a bullet from the opposite shore hit it with a dull clunk. Instantly, three M-1 rifles fired back at the ruins. Donnelly looked quickly inside the hole he'd uncovered, then turned and hobbled back to the warehouse, trying to ignore the throbbing in his foot.

Not a single mortar shell had been fired at him, just the few scattered shots, which meant the Jerries were still setting up.

"You were right," Donnelly said breathlessly. "There's a ledge on top of some pilings. It's stacked with burp guns, rat guns, grenades and ammunition. Those manholes give easy access to the ledge, so all those bastards have to do is reach our side and pull the stuff out and start shooting. They couldn't break the First Battalion's lines to get their generals out before they left, so they did the next best thing: they tried to assure themselves a quick, easy return trip when they came to get their pigs out of the hospital."

Kaplan looked perplexed. "But, sir, how could they be sure our First Battalion wouldn't come over the bridge after them?"

"The German civilians must have observed First Battalion preparing to leave the way they came in—seen our G.I.'s forming into columns rather than battle formations, assembling their gear, loading up trucks.... Only the rear guard kept fighting, and these Krauts are anything but stupid. They passed word to the German troops that First Battalion wasn't planning to cross the river."

"So that's why they held up the battalion so long," said Kaplan. "They had to keep us from actually getting to the riverbank while they stashed their arms."

Donnelly nodded. "But now they've seen me lift the lid. They know we're onto them."

"Think they'll try a hurry-up attack across the bridge?"

Charles shook his head. "It's broad daylight. We'd slaughter them."

"So they'll try to slip a few men over to do the job tonight."

"Could be..." Donnelly said doubtfully. "But they'll need stretchers to carry their pigs out. Can't just sneak them out of town. We control everything west of the river. They'll have to get back across the bridge, to the east." Charles sat down on a workbench to take the weight off his foot, the pain now a hot knife. "No, they have to capture the hospital and gain complete control of the town if they're going to get their generals out. That means eliminating any American troops on this side of the Main. And despite our success last night, I'm afraid they still have us heavily outnumbered and outgunned."

"It doesn't look good, does it, sir?"

"We have to get the generals out of that hospital now. It's our only chance." Donnelly leaned out the window and shouted toward the building down the street.

"Grant! You're in charge here at the bridge until I get back. Kaplan and I will be at the hospital."

★

By the light of day, the hospital looked less sinister than it had the night before. The rusty padlock had disappeared. In its place, two of Kaplan's men stood guard at the big double doors. Charles and Kaplan had seen no sign of civilians as they had walked through the streets of Belingen. But Charles felt their eyes on them. He wished that some or even one of the locals would cross the river and notify the Nazis after the SS generals were taken from the hospital, but he knew this was an impossibility. Somehow, he'd have to convince the German soldiers that the generals were gone—otherwise they would surely storm the town and try to rescue them.

Charles quietly opened the door and entered the antiseptic-smelling reception hall, its floor wide, tiled in black and white marble squares. Doric columns marked the bottom of a wide staircase that led to the balcony and the hospital rooms beyond. As they stood there in the empty hall, a large bearded man in a threadbare suit and white lab coat approached from around a corner.

"*Ja?*"

"Doctor," Donnelly said briskly, "we've come for the SS generals."

"Eine moment, bitte. No speak English." He looked up at the balcony and called loudly. "Marie! *Kommen sie hier, bitte!"*

Donnelly put his hand on his pistol and Kaplan clicked off the safety of his M-1 as they waited to see who might appear. Was it really a translator, or were German soldiers hiding upstairs, waiting to ambush them? As they stood there, looking up, a woman appeared, the sunlight behind her creating a halo around her head. Donnelly gasped, as he gazed at the angel from his dream last night.

But if he had met her before she didn't seem to remember. She came down the stairs and walked over, looking at him blandly with her large brown eyes, before turning to talk with the doctor.

"Doctor Watville is the superintendent of the hospital. He does not speak English," she explained to Donnelly. "He asks to know why you have come. We have already given you our much-needed supplies. We have no more to give," she said brusquely.

"We've come for the German officers," Donnelly answered sternly. "Do you have an ambulance we can use to take them away? And don't pretend they're not here. I saw them myself last night."

As she translated, Doctor Watville nodded.

"Ja," she said. "The doctor says they are here, and you may take them away. He already has enough trouble. He is not interested in this war, only in his patients. You may have the ambulance. But we have no benzine. No petrol."

"I think I can fix that." Donnelly turned to Kaplan. "Terry, get a couple of men to bring over two or three jerry cans of gasoline. I'll stay here and arrange for the evacuation of the generals. And we'll need a couple of your men to ride back with them."

While the doctor spoke rapidly to his nurse, Charles waited, admiring the nurse's thick brown hair framing a porcelain doll face. He swore he could smell the scent of lilac soap even from two feet away.

"Herr Doctor Watville asks me to make clear to you that he is not helping you. You are threatening to kill him if he does not give you the ambulance, *ja?* If the German troops return, this is

what they, and everyone else in this hospital, must think. There are many spies here."

"Tell him the German soldiers will not return."

The doctor looked skeptical as she translated. He answered her slowly.

"What is he saying?" Donnelly asked.

"He says the German soldiers always return. He says he does not have much hope left, but what little supplies he has he gives to you. And he says be careful. The walls here have many ears."

Donnelly turned to Doctor Watville to thank him, but the superintendent had already disappeared down the corridor.

"Let us go to the officers," the nurse said. She turned and walked briskly up the wide staircase without waiting for Donnelly.

He hurried to catch up with her. "What is their condition?"

"They will need immediate medical attention from your doctors."

"Will they survive the journey out of here?"

"Yes. Most certainly, I am sorry to say." She stopped on the balcony.

"Please draw your gun and place it in my back, Captain."

Charles looked at her blandly.

"Now!" she said urgently, as a hospital worker came down the hall toward them. "Civilian," she whispered. They waited until the man had passed. "He will report what he has seen to the Gestapo." The nurse led Donnelly down the hallway to the room he had been in last night. "I will wait for you out here." Charles opened the door and looked in to make sure that the generals were still there. Satisfied, he tiptoed out without waking them. When the time came, he would have them carried out on stretchers by hospital staff. Until the last possible moment, he wanted them to think they were being rescued rather than taken prisoner. The element of surprise might deter an attempted ambush, at least until the ambulance was safely away.

The nurse stood in the hallway, absently sweeping a loose strand of dark hair behind her ear.

"Is there someplace I can wait until my men return? Someplace we can talk safely?"

"You can wait in my office. There, no one will bother us."

Her office turned out to be a storeroom on the first floor. A small desk hunched in a corner; mops, buckets, and shelves of cleaners taking up most of her cramped space.

"Cozy," Donnelly offered.

She forced a smile. "The Superintendent lets me use this room for myself. Many nights I slept at the hospital. Though we had little left to offer them, the wounded came from everywhere before you captured the town."

Charles sat with one leg dangling over the corner of the small desk. The nurse stood, uncertain whether to leave or to stay.

"You are not from around here," Charles said, looking at her directly for the first time. She was not the blonde, blue-eyed Germanic type at all. Still, thought Charles, very beautiful, indeed.

"I come from Alsace. We speak German as well as French," she said. "The Germans occupied Alsace from 1870 to 1918. They returned in 1940."

Charles nodded. It wasn't what the girl said, but the charming way she said it, that stirred a passion in him he'd never felt before. And her eyes were so large, her lips so full, her figure as close to perfection as anything he'd ever seen. He smiled at her and she smiled back.

"You are wondering why I am working for the Germans. I married two years ago, in 1943. The Germans took my husband three weeks later and put him in the army." She paused and breathed deeply. "I never saw him again. He was killed in Russia."

Charles instinctively reached out and took her hand. His sympathy was genuine, and the girl seemed to realize it. Slowly she curled her fingers around his.

"I had trained as a nurse. After my husband was killed, I decided to join the staff of our local hospital. One day the

Germans came and took most of us to serve in their army hospitals. Doctor Watville was also taken. And so, you see, I am here."

As she spoke, Charles found himself staring at her openly. It was the way her mouth formed words, the way she held herself and the body motions she made. Her cheeks, he noted, were a charming shade of pink, and her nose turned upwards slightly. She reminded him of a beautiful movie star; not any particular star, just a gorgeous one. It was several seconds before he realized that she had stopped talking and was simply returning his gaze. He could feel his cheeks redden. He fumbled for words. "I was just thinking.... Well, never mind. I'm sorry, what were you saying?"

"It is all right," she said gently. There was a long pause.

Charles said awkwardly. "I'm Charles Donnelly."

"I am Marie Dumont. But I think we have met, no? How is your heel? You were in a lot of pain last night."

His eyes widened and without thinking, he reached out and took her other hand. "So it really was you."

She bowed her head. "Yes."

Donnelly looked away. "I'm afraid I must have sounded a bit silly."

"Actually," Marie said smiling, "it was the nicest conversation I've had in a long time."

Charles looked up, surprised. "The funny thing is, I meant every word I said."

"Are you sure you weren't just delirious?"

"I was delirious, but not from the pain."

"I'm glad."

"Can I see you tonight?" he whispered.

Marie remained silent.

"I'm sorry, I don't mean to be forward. But who knows what will happen tomorrow?"

Marie dropped her eyes and nodded shyly.

"Ten o'clock. I'll be outside."

They were interrupted by Kaplan's voice, calling for Donnelly. Charles opened the door and waved. "Over here!"

"Oh, there you are, Captain. The ambulance is full of gasoline. We're ready to roll."

"Good work." Charles turned to Marie. "I have to go load the generals." Halfway out the door, he stopped. He looked back at her openly and she returned his gaze without embarrassment.

"Thank you for taking care of me last night," he said.

"It is my job," she answered. "But even if it was not—"

Charles interrupted, "Please, Marie, be very careful."

She nodded.

11

It had been a brutal day, and Donnelly longed to throw himself onto a pile of blankets to get some sleep. Instead, he found himself limping through the deserted streets of Belingen toward the hospital. Why am I doing this? he wondered. Why? But even as he asked himself the question he knew the answer. Despite the danger—both to himself and Marie—he had to, simply had to, see her again.

Earlier that day, Captain Donnelly had brought Superintendent Watville, Marie, and a group of doctors down to the river under a white flag, and they had informed the leaders of the SS troops across the Main, through Marie's translation, that their generals had been taken out of town by the Americans. It was the first time Charles had actually seen his enemy by daylight. The one thing he noticed was their black SS collars. By their tone of voice, they sounded nasty, and they seemed unconvinced. Charles worried that they might try to slip a patrol in force over the river that night to find out for themselves. If they did, he should be with his men, not with Marie. His emotions of duty and of ardor were fighting a gigantic battle inside him. Finally, he dismissed the idea of the SS bastards trying to come back.

Now, walking quietly in the shadows, Charles reached the hospital. He stopped in the square and stood in the shadow of an oak tree where he could see the hospital staff come and go. The blackout curtains were drawn, and no light shone from the door or the windows. Darkness, unlike any he'd experienced in civilian life engulfed the town.

He could barely make out his watch dial. Ten o'clock exactly. He stared at the hospital door, willing it to open, willing Marie to appear. He propped himself against the tree and waited.

"Hello, Captain Donnelly." Even though the words were whispered, they made Donnelly jump. They came from behind him. He spun around.

There was a rustle in the foliage behind him. Marie appeared still wearing her white nurse's uniform with a dark cloak over her shoulders. She seemed so clean and fresh-looking that she made Donnelly aware of how incongruous he must appear in his torn, stained battle gear, a web belt around his waist with its .45 pistol, first-aid kit and canteen, a dirty, bandaged bare foot and dusty combat boot, his steel helmet dented and black, his face unshaven. Had he taken the time to clean up, one of his men might have asked what he was up to. Even though he knew that some of them had formed liaisons with certain German civilians in the cellars of the town, he didn't want them to know what he was doing. He didn't know why. After all, human beings are human beings.

Marie radiated delight. The urgency of war does not allow time for either coquetry or courtship. Without a word, she stepped toward him and wrapped herself in his arms.

His lips mingled with her hair.

Marie took his hand. "This way," she whispered. She led him to a large apartment house a half a block away. They stopped in a stairwell across the street from the building.

"Wait." She darted out, and, looking both ways, unlocked the front door of the building. When she was sure that the coast was clear, she beckoned him.

Wordlessly, Charles followed Marie down a stuffy, unlit hallway. He couldn't see his own hands in front of him. As she opened the door to her room, he listened carefully. He thought he heard a floorboard creak somewhere in the darkness. He drew his .45. A hand reached out and pulled him into the room. "You do not need this gun."

"I'm sorry," Charles said hastily.

"It's all right," Marie replied. "You have no choice but to be cautious."

Charles listened to Marie moving around the room, checking the blackout curtains to make sure they were securely fastened. Satisfied, she lit a kerosene lamp, and the small wood-burning stove, on which she placed a kettle of water. The light revealed a simple room: a threadbare couch and a chest of drawers pushed up against one wall; in a small alcove on the other side of the room stood a feather bed and a low bookcase. A red and white cloth covered a wooden table to the left. Right in the middle of the room stood an enormous claw-footed bathtub.

Marie followed Charles's gaze. "Such a silly thing to have, I know. There is no room for it," she shrugged. "And, of course, I don't have enough water to fill it."

Charles turned his head from side to side, taking in the clean, crisp, slightly perfumed scent of the room. "It's the nicest place I've been in a long, long time," he said, moving toward her. Then, remembering, he stopped, removed his helmet, unhooked the web belt holding his .45 and laid them on the floor.

When he stood up, she had moved close to him. He put his arms around her waist and leaned down to kiss her upturned face. She kissed him back, gently at first, then with growing desire. Their warm, young bodies were as one.

Finally, she broke away. "You must be tired. You fought hard today, no?"

"I was tired but not anymore. I wish I could have cleaned up but..."

"I have an idea," she said, moving to the stove where the kettle of water was already heating. "Take off your coat and shirt."

When she returned, Donnelly had removed his field jacket and stripped to the waist. Wordlessly she unbuttoned his trousers and unwrapped the bandage on his foot. Then he helped her out of her uniform, kissing her hard. When he eased her toward the bed, she hesitated and whispered breathlessly, "Wait... not yet."

She led him to the bath. "There is no water to fill the tub... You'll have to pretend."

He sank down in the bath as Marie slowly poured the warm water from the kettle over his shoulders and back. Soapy hands followed, massaging his neck and back, moving fluidly over his chest. As her hands moved downwards, Marie sensed their shared urgency and quickly rinsed him off. Then, dripping wet, he stepped out of the bath, dried himself hurriedly with a threadbare towel and carried her to the bed. Without waiting, she took the initiative. Charles groaned with pleasure. She made love to him fast and hard until the world outside completely receded. Rolling her over, Charles came, gasping for breath. Marie moaned softly, and rested her head back against the pillow.

"I love you," Charles said.

"I know," she said smiling. "You told me after I bandaged your foot."

He leaned closer and whispered in her ear, "Marie, if I survive this war, I—"

"Shhh," she purred softly. "In wartime, there are no promises."

He understood what she meant and kept quiet. Charles did not know how long they lay like that, locked inside each other. But at some point he felt Marie shiver with renewed pleasure. He stroked her hair and kissed her everywhere. His hands enjoyed the perfection of her naked body. Charles could feel himself getting aroused all over again.

"I need you inside me," she whispered. "It washes the pain away."

They stayed in bed for several more hours, whispering sweet words. Several times, they dozed together then awoke suddenly, hungry for each other again.

Deep into the night, not long before dawn, Donnelly sensed it was time to go. He didn't know if he could do it, but he had to tear himself away from Marie. He dressed quickly. Sitting up on the edge of the bed, he gazed lovingly at her naked body. Long and lithe with firm breasts capped with small red nipples, angelic eyes and wide soft lips. Around her neck, she wore a silver chain, which held a tiny ring.

He reached out and fingered the ring. There was something familiar about it. It was a simple, inexpensive silver band with two roses entwined on the front.

"Where did you get this?" Charles asked abruptly.

Marie sighed. "I bought it in Paris. Nothing fancy. My best friend and I went there when we were sixteen. It was a kind of friendship ring to commemorate the journey. We vowed to wear the ring all our lives. But my fingers grew too big..."

Charles's stomach turned. "What is her name?" he asked feebly.

She looked puzzled. "Isabelle Foche. Why? Where did that question come from?"

Charles shook his head. "It doesn't make sense."

Marie sighed, then sat up on the bed beside him. "Charles, I cannot keep secrets from you. While I was in the French resistance, I was recruited by allied intelligence to work for them."

"What? Then why didn't you tell our people about the SS dogs in the hospital?"

"I did. At great risk to myself, I told the major commanding your troops here. He was too occupied with chasing the Boche across the Main, then moving on to some sort of assault down the river. He didn't want to bother about the SS generals."

"You're an intelligence officer?" he asked incredulously.

She nodded gravely. "And Isabelle too."

Oh God, Donnelly thought. It can't be.

"I received word through one of our couriers. My friend, Isabelle, had reconnoitered the German positions and was supposed to meet an American task force when they crossed the Rhine above

Oppenheim." Marie's voice caught in her throat. "I haven't heard anything from her or about her since. I think she must have been killed during a bombardment."

Charles felt sick. "She was an allied agent sent to help us?"

Marie cocked her head. "Yes, of course. Charles, you're scaring me. What's wrong?"

He wrapped his arm around her and said softly, "Marie, I'm sorry. Your friend was brutally murdered by one of our officers. I saw her body... and the ring."

Marie gasped. A tear rolled down her face. "But why?" she asked.

Charles decided not to tell her the simple, stupid truth—not yet anyway. Instead, he asked, "Do you have any idea who she was supposed to contact on the other side of the Rhine?"

She shook her head, tears streaming down her cheeks now. "No. I knew very little. But it would be usual to make the initial rendezvous with your intelligence officer."

"Good God!" exclaimed Charles. Johnny? he thought. No. Impossible.

"You know the man, then."

Charles looked up in a daze. "Yes. He was very upset when he saw the body." He remembered John's reaction when he first saw the girl lying there.

Marie shook her head. She said, "Only a German would want to kill Isabelle. She was their enemy, not yours."

"It's more complicated than that, I'm afraid."

Marie went silent. "How did he kill her?" she asked finally.

"Slit her throat with a Bowie knife."

"When you find him, do the same thing to him. For me, Charles."

"I think he's already dead. He was no good. Somebody caught him killing Isabelle and shot him dead." He was concerned about St. John. Could he possibly have murdered Ames in cold blood? If he'd caught him raping Isabelle, yes, he probably would have.

"I hear something," Marie whispered suddenly.

Now Charles, too, could hear a commotion outside. "What is it?"

"German voices," she said, visibly scared. "I think it is the SS."

She sat up in bed. Her lovely breasts clearly visible, rising and falling as she breathed. He saw her nipples harden again.

Charles nodded. "Stay in bed. Don't go outside. I'll come back. If not tonight, then before I leave. I prom—"

She stopped him, pressing her lips to his. He kissed her passionately and held her to him. Then he extinguished the lamp and slipped out the door.

Barefoot, he limped noiselessly down the street. In his left hand he carried his one combat boot. He stopped at the corner and carefully peered around. Two German officers stood in front of the hospital whispering insistently to the doctors inside. They were well armed. Both had pistols in holsters, one had a submachine gun as well. Charles put down his boot and drew his .45 pistol from its holster. He crept closer to the hospital steps.

The German officers clearly wanted to get inside, but the doors were strongly barred now, on Charles's orders. They think their generals are still there, Charles realized.

He was sorry now that he'd removed the guards from the hospital, but there didn't seem to be any reason to keep them there since the generals had gone. Inching forward, he waited for the right moment then ran toward them, his .45 in hand.

"Raise your hands!" he shouted. At that moment, Charles's bare toe struck the first step and he tripped. He fell to his knees, completely off balance. One of the German officers reached for his pistol, the other began to unsling his submachine gun.

Charles threw himself onto the steps, aimed his .45 and fired at almost the exact instant the two Germans did. He beat them by a fraction of a second, hitting each squarely, hurling them against the side of the hospital building. Three shots had been fired by the Germans in an after-death reflex. Their bullets spanged off the concrete stairs throwing up clouds of cement dust. Charles rose to his feet. "Go back to bed," he ordered the doctors through the shut wooden door. "The SS officers are *kaput*."

Charles pulled on his boot. Then he wiped his hands on the pavement and rubbed dirt into his face and hair. He didn't want to look as if he had just stepped out of a bath. The firing would have alerted his men and they'd be on their way by now.

Moments later the sound of running feet broke the silence of the night.

"Hey!" called Charles. The men stopped.

"Captain Donnelly?" It was Kaplan. "What are you doing here?"

"I was waiting for these bastards," lied Charles. "I figured they'd show up sooner or later. I knew they wouldn't believe that we'd really shipped their top pigs out of town. These officers wouldn't come alone. I'm pretty certain they've got a task force on our side of the river and they'll be here soon."

"What are our orders?" Kaplan asked.

Donnelly's mind raced. He couldn't think of a way to protect the town against an attack on this side of the Main and still keep a force at the river to prevent a crossing. "How active are the Krauts at the river tonight?"

"They lob in about three to five mortar shells an hour," answered Kaplan.

"Do we shoot back?"

"Sometimes. It depends whether or not Grant is asleep. When he's awake, he likes to fire the light .30 at them."

"Okay, good," said Donnelly. "Now, listen to me and listen closely. We have to work fast."

"They're coming. They're coming." The scout raced back to Captain Donnelly, who waited under the large tree near the hospital. "Two columns up that street there," he said, pointing.

Donnelly turned to Terry Kaplan, who stood with his riflemen behind a building. "Get your men into those second-story rooms along this side of the street."

The men moved quickly and quietly into the houses.

"Grant," said Donnelly. "Set up your light .30 where it can do the most damage when we open up."

Grant nodded and gave orders to his men, who immediately began assembling the machine gun at the side of another building. From their position, they could hit anything that came down the street.

Donnelly's ambush had been ready only a few seconds when the Germans came trotting down the road in perfect formation, their rifles held at high port, their eyes searching the semi-darkness for signs of snipers. For a fleeting moment, Donnelly admired their arrogance. But standing beside Grant's machine gun, he didn't hesitate. The first German was ten yards away when Donnelly's arm came slashing down. Grant's machine gun let loose a long, chattering burst, and the rifles from the windows of the buildings were popping everywhere, interspersed with the explosions of hand grenades tossed into the street.

The slaughter lasted less than a minute.

"Stop! Stop!" Donnelly shouted.

The machine gun's clatter ceased at once; the popping of the rifles eased off until an eerie silence filled the street. Except for the piles of bodies, which lined both sides of the pavement, the street was empty. But Donnelly had seen a few enemy soldiers at the rear of the columns scurry out of the line of fire.

"Okay," he yelled, getting his men's attention. "Let's go chase the rest of these pricks out of town."

Before the words were even out of his mouth, he was hobbling down the street as fast as he could. Behind him, he heard his riflemen stomping down the stairs and into the street.

At the first corner, Donnelly slowed, sure he had seen a shadow disappear into a building just ahead. But he couldn't hear a thing besides the 57 banging away. He had ordered the antitank gun to keep firing to make the Jerries on the other side of the river keep their heads down as long as the fighting continued on the west bank. Carefully hugging the wall, Donnelly looked inside the building. Nothing but an empty hallway. The shadow had disappeared. He could see no other exits. The rising sun must have been playing tricks with the light. Outside, riflemen clattered past him in pursuit of the retreating Germans.

Terry Kaplan stopped on the street beside Donnelly. "Are you all right, sir?" he asked, as the last rifleman disappeared down the road.

"I thought I saw someone come in here, but it was nothing."

A shot rang out, and Donnelly looked up just in time to see a rifle barrel disappear into an upper-story window across the street as Kaplan slumped into his arms.

Keeping his eyes on the window, Donnelly lowered Kaplan gently to the ground. He felt for a heartbeat. Nothing.

Rage welled in Donnelly's gut.

He snatched Kaplan's rifle from the ground and ran across the street into the building on the other side. He bounded up the stairs and burst into a room on the second floor facing the street. Beside the window, sitting on a low chair, an old man held an antique gun, which was already aimed at the door. A teenaged boy with a blond crewcut knelt beside him loading a high-powered hunting rifle. Charles had just enough time to notice the huge black swastikas painted on every wall before the old man's rifle blasted at him. Luckily, the powder in the shot was as old as the gun and the bullet ricocheted off his helmet. Charles stood in the door, dazed and confused, as the boy handed the old man the loaded rifle. As he began to swing the muzzle toward Donnelly, Charles suddenly remembered that he held Kaplan's M-1. Without thinking, he fired from the hip, killing the two civilians instantly. The boy was about the same age as Kaplan, Charles thought numbly, as he walked out of the room.

Back in the street, Charles knelt beside Terry. He took off his field jacket and placed it over Kaplan's face and chest. In the distance he could hear his riflemen firing at the last of the SS on this side of the river.

How I hate this wretched war, Donnelly thought. An involuntary tear splashed down his cheek.

By mid-afternoon Donnelly's men still held their side of the Main. They received word that American troops had crossed the river, but hadn't been able to break out. Donnelly had to hold on until they did.

But he had lost more than half of his men, and his ammunition was down to a few rounds. The machine gun was completely out. Just after Kaplan had been killed, some of Miller's men had seen the Germans putting a boat into the river upstream. Glen Miller had brought his gun out of cover to get a better angle of fire on them, and just as he had secured a position, the Germans had plastered the whole damned area with mortar shells. It had been an obvious set up, and if Charles had been there he would have ordered Miller to stay out of sight. But he had been with Kaplan, and by the time he reached the river it was too late. Glen Miller and all of his men were dead.

Charles sat at his command post window staring blankly across the river. He had lost two of his three sergeants, and far too many of his men. He had failed as a captain and leader. Reason told him that the death count was not his fault—men die in war. But his heart felt otherwise. If only he had seen Kaplan's sniper upstairs instead of a fleeting shadow. If only he had reached the river faster. And still, he wondered how long he could keep the Germans away. Any minute now they would realize he had nothing left but a few riflemen.

Charles forced himself to get up from his chair. He tested his foot. The pain was almost gone now. No doubt the healing process had been helped by Marie's care and a clean bandage. He imagined Marie was at the hospital now. Had anyone seen her with him? If he and his men didn't make it through the day, the Germans would immediately storm the hospital, looking for news of their generals. They would flush out any traitors. Somehow, he had to make sure that didn't happen.

Charles pulled on his jacket, stained dark crimson with Kaplan's blood. He was halfway out the door when, without warning, American artillery shells screamed overhead. He had a split second of fear for his men and for himself, before the shells began smashing into the rubble on the German-held side of the river. That could only mean one thing. The troops would not be far behind.

Sure enough, as soon as the big guns stopped firing, Charles heard the popping of M-ls, the reassuring rhythm of Browning Automatic Rifles, the stuttering of light machine guns. German automatic weapons answered back, and Charles could hear the cracking of Mausers and the hollow blasting of German grenades. But gradually these sounds diminished until it was all M-ls, B.A.R.'s and American grenades. The German troops had been whipped.

By God, it was finally over.

Charles leaned against a brick wall and breathed a heavy sigh of relief. Outnumbered by more than twenty to one, his three small squads had beaten back a battalion-strength, elite enemy unit. But the men he had lost could never be replaced. Kaplan, Miller, and so many more... all brave young soldiers, all dead.

As evening fell, Donnelly and Montana sat in their Jeep at the river's edge gazing out across the water. Only two afternoons ago, they had sat on the hill overlooking Belingen, waiting to move into the now-battered town.

Wistfully, Charles looked toward the hospital. He wanted desperately to see Marie again before leaving Belingen. He had promised he would. But there was no time now. At least he'd been able to send Olsen to the hospital with a sealed note addressed to Madame Dumont, letting her know that he was all right. He told her again that he loved her, that he would always love her. He hoped that, between the lines, Marie would read what he really wanted to write—that he would come back for her, no matter what.

In wartime, there are no promises, she had said. And she was right.

"What now, sir?" Montana's voice startled him out of his musing.

He wondered how to answer. In the town of Belingen on the Main, Charles Donnelly had known true love for the first time in his life. Only now, at the age of twenty-five, did he feel he truly had something… someone… to live for. It filled him with dread for this terrible war—and a will to survive it that he had never known before.

What now, Montana had asked. Without turning, Charles said, "We'll keep on going as long as we can survive, or until we've killed every German in front of us...."

On the far side of the river, the smoke began to dissipate, and the dust settled. With the battle over, civilians emerged from their cellars. Women took one look at their ravaged town and reached for their brooms to sweep the streets. Old men piled chunks of rubble into neat pyramids. Far in the distance, Charles could hear the faint booming of cannon, or was it a thunderstorm a long way off?

Captain Charles Donnelly took a slow, deep breath. For now, he felt out of danger, even relaxed. It was not a feeling he had experienced often in this war.

12

On returning to headquarters, Charles Donnelly found he had a letter from his mother. Fairly recent, he noted. Her letters always made him smile. He decided to read it before reporting to the colonel and provoking the unpleasant scene he knew would ensue. The gist of this letter was that his father was outstanding in his new magisterial authority and looked like a king in his judicial robes. His brother David's girl had tried out for, and gotten, a movie part and now went under the stage name of Hillary Grant. "Wouldn't it be marvelous if she became a movie star and David married her?" Charles shook his head and smiled. That the same girl could be "most undesirable" one day and a most suitable wife for his brother the next, illustrated something, but he wasn't sure what. Muffy's husband, his mother was sad to say, had died unexpectedly of a sudden, massive heart attack. Then it turned out that instead of being a fabulously rich millionaire, he was broke and heavily in debt. She went on to say that, as Charles knew, Muffy was from a fine family who lost all their money in the crash of 1929, but her mother's family still had enough to live on, thankfully. Then, there was the baby. "Most people feel that with her good looks, Muffy will be married again soon." Had Charles written to express his condolences? Condolences? thought Charles. I just this minute learned the news.

It occurred to him he was in the middle of two worlds. One, the sane world as described by his mother's letters—where chorus girls became movie stars, great lawyers became greater judges, broke tycoons dropped dead, and their widows started husband hunting. Dramatic, sure, but rare events in the normal everyday lives of the citizens of the United States. Exceptional enough to write about in a letter to a son.

The other world, his world—where you could die any second, where buildings and whole towns got blown to pieces, and men were slaughtered like cattle, where you lived in mortal fear twenty-four hours a day and thanked God when a red-hot jagged piece of steel missed your head by inches, where you slept in the snow in the winter and went without food so you could carry more ammunition, where you grabbed an hour of sleep never knowing whether or not you'd ever wake up, where you killed men you didn't even know, just to keep them from killing you.... Which was the real world? They both were—at least for now. Charles knew he hated his world and longed for the other. But how long does peace last? Unless something unusual happened, he figured another twenty-five years or so. And the next war would be worse, much worse. They'd use that twenty-five years to develop more efficient methods to kill people, just as they had since the last war. To hell with it. Live from day to day like every other infantry soldier.

✪

Major Ramon Gonzalez-Rivera flicked a speck of dust off the cuff of his sleeve. He prided himself on being neatly groomed and cleanly attired at all times—a rare achievement under the strain of war.

Sitting at his desk in the new regimental headquarters, now located in a warehouse building east of the Main, the major leaned back in his chair and yawned.

As Gonzalez-Rivera stared idly out the window, a tall, well-built colonel entered Ramon's office unannounced. He handed an envelope to Gonzalez-Rivera, who read it, nodded to the colonel, then lit a match and burned the envelope and its contents until they were nothing but ashes in his metal wastepaper basket.

"You know who I am," said the colonel.

"Of course, sir. I'd recognize you by sight anyplace."

"Good. But I would prefer it if nobody else knows who I am until our mission is over.

"Colonel Coleman?"

"He knows who I am and where we're going. He has no idea at all what our real mission is, and I want to keep it that way."

"I think I should mention, sir, that we have an ongoing murder investigation in progress," said Ramon. "I am a suspect, for some reason or other."

"We'll fix it."

"Thank you, sir."

"Any idea who did it?"

"No, sir."

"Who's heading the investigation?"

"A captain named Donnelly."

"Why? Why isn't St. John in charge?"

"You already know an awful lot about our unit, Colonel."

"I know General Marks's son was murdered. I also know Captain St. John is your intelligence officer and has an I.Q. that's stratospheric. So who is Donnelly?"

"A good officer. Probably the best combat officer I know. Has the D.S.C., a bucketful of Purple Hearts and is about to get the Medal of Honor. Coleman picked him because he was in law school when he got drafted."

"Sounds fishy. Could Coleman be covering up something?"

"Not likely, sir. Coleman's nephew was the first one murdered."

"A good combat man like Donnelly could do murder without a qualm. Do you think he did? Does Coleman think he did?"

"No, sir." Then Ramon paused. "But, then again, Coleman sent Donnelly into a pretty sticky one recently. He had to hold a town against five hundred SS officer candidates. Coleman gave Donnelly less than thirty men to do the job."

The colonel waved his hand to indicate he'd lost interest in the murder investigation.

Ramon nodded, signifying his agreement. Then abruptly he asked, "Where is Hechingen?"

"About fifty miles south of Stuttgart."

"That's behind enemy lines."

"If it wasn't behind enemy lines, we wouldn't need Task Force Coleman to get us there," snapped the unnamed colonel.

"Of course," Gonzalez-Rivera said smoothly. "And please let me assure you, sir, we will get what we're after."

✪

The door to Coleman's office flung open. Without glancing up from his work, Coleman said, "I've been thinking, Ramon, suppose I refuse to take these men along until I'm—"

"It's not Gonzalez-Rivera. It's me. Reporting in from Belingen."

Coleman swung around. He held out his hand. "Charles, Charles, my boy, I can't tell you how pleased I am that you're back." He smiled.

Donnelly did not smile back. As he walked forward he limped. His left shoe was off and a bandage covered his foot. "I couldn't save Terry Kaplan's life," he said angrily. "Or Glen Miller's. Or the others who died."

Coleman looked shocked. "Charles."

"They were all good men, sir." Charles could feel himself losing control and took a few deep breaths. "What the hell were you thinking when you sent me in with a handful of men against five hundred crack SS storm troops? I felt like Uriah out there."

Coleman stood up indignantly. "Pull yourself together, soldier, or you'll be facing a general court-martial and twenty years in Leavenworth. And who the hell is Uriah?"

Charles smiled sardonically. "Uriah, sir, was a soldier, the husband of Bathsheba. King David also loved Bathsheba so he sent

Uriah to the front line of battle where he was sure to be killed. And he was, sir."

"Settle down, Donnelly. I'm sorry about what happened. I didn't know about the Nazi generals. No one did. I thought you'd just be keeping the Jerries on the other side of the river pinned down. I had no idea how many there were, or that they'd try to cross."

"They wouldn't leave their generals behind," Charles said dully.

"Headquarters and the press are making a big thing of their capture. They're making a hero out of you. You'll get the Medal of Honor for this."

"St. John deserves the credit." He wondered what would happen if the most improbable had taken place, and Johnny killed Ames.

"St. John?" Coleman seemed confused. "What does he have to do with Belingen? He wasn't near the place."

"If it hadn't been for Johnny, we'd all be dead. He brought in artillery. He's the one who found the generals."

"In that case, I'll overlook the fact that he acted without my knowledge. And I'm glad he did. You are here, you are alive, and your mission was a success."

Charles collapsed in a chair opposite the colonel. "Was it?"

"Was it what, Donnelly?"

"A success. I failed to keep my men alive. What kind of a success is that?"

"This is war, Charles. Even in our small sector, hundreds of our men die every day."

Charles nodded somberly.

"It's the business we're in, Charles. You've lost men before. You had all three of your antitank guns knocked out during the Bulge. You lost men after that, too."

"I know. I guess I was so busy playing detective, that I forgot why I was really here." He sighed heavily. "Sir, I'd like those bullets now. As soon as I get cleaned up, I'll take them over to C.I.D."

"Of course. I'll get them for you." Coleman walked across the room and unlocked a door that led into an inner office.

Charles closed his eyes and listened to the click of metal and the rustle of papers as the strongbox was opened. He wasn't even sure that he wanted to know the results.

A minute later Coleman reappeared with the folded envelopes. He handed them to Charles. "I had a letter from my sister," he said quietly. "She is so filled with grief she could barely write. I think she'll have a nervous breakdown. Just a matter of time."

"I'm sorry, sir."

"We've got to find the killer, Charles. I promised her."

"Yes, sir," Charles answered. "I made a similar promise myself." He waved the envelopes in a token salute and headed for the door.

Coleman saluted casually. "Safe journey, Captain."

The following day, Donnelly slid quietly through the back door of a large room where Colonel Coleman was briefing his battalion and company commanders. Charles visited the hospital when he went to the rear and, thanks to some special new bandages, now wore both combat boots.

"We're moving out, gentleman," Coleman announced. "We're spearheading the Seventh Army. Our objective is Hechingen."

In a quick second of eye contact, Donnelly gave Coleman a thumbs-up. Mission accomplished. Montana had broken all the speed records in the book enabling Charles to deliver the bullets personally that morning, and still make it to the hospital.

Coleman continued, "The town is fifty miles south of Stuttgart. This means it is behind enemy lines. Our mission, besides the usual advance, is to deliver this group of soldiers who just joined us to Hechingen."

"Sir, what's between Stuttgart and Hechingen?" another officer asked.

"We aren't sure," said Coleman. "It's still held by the enemy, but we're expecting some intelligence reports now."

Paul Turner raised his hand. "Why's it so damned important to take this town, Colonel? On my map, it ain't no big deal. It don't control nothing."

"I don't know, Paul. What I do know is this: The army wants that town, and they want it yesterday. Any more questions before we get down to the details of our route of march and order of battle?"

The room fell silent.

"Okay, here it is. We're going completely motorized. The trucks are assembling now, and we move out at midnight so as to arrive in occupied territory in daylight..."

Donnelly paced back and forth nervously. Once again, he checked the back of the Jeep to make sure he hadn't forgotten anything. Where was St. John? They were supposed to be leaving ahead of the others to reconnoiter in front of the truck column. But it was already eleven thirty, and still St. John had not appeared. Donnelly was anxious. What would he do when he saw St. John? How would he act, knowing that Johnny had been Isabelle's contact? Then, he thought back to the Rhine. Hearing about the rape and murder of Isabelle had almost driven the usually nonchalant St. John crazy. John had been delayed by his assignment to the minefield fiasco. The delay had caused him to be late for his rendezvous with Isabelle. Charles nodded in the dark. He relaxed, knowing his friend, Johnny, was in the clear. Now, once again, he really did want to know the results of the tests.

Suddenly, there were footsteps on the gravel road behind him. "Dammit, Johnny, it's about time."

"Take it easy. It's only me." Gonzalez-Rivera materialized out of the darkness. "Are you all set, Donnelly?" he asked. As usual, he was checking to make sure the soldiers were ready and supplies in order. Gonzalez-Rivera was always the last to leave. He had to give the Command Post they were abandoning a final inspection; then he'd follow the column and help out any stragglers with engine problems or other difficulties. He had apparently completed his inspection, for he plopped down in the driver's seat as though he had all the time in the world.

After a long silence, Charles took the other seat, looked over and said, "You have something to do with this mission, don't you, sir? The men we're taking to Hechingen aren't your regular soldiers. They're older men, they're educated and cultivated. They stick to themselves. They're—they're just out of place, Major."

"Yes," Gonzalez-Rivera mused, "they're not your usual soldiers. So tell me, Donnelly, who do you think they are?"

Charles didn't hesitate. "I think they're here to investigate the murders of Ames and Marks."

"You're probably right."

"So why are they assigned to you, Major? You're not a policeman."

Gonzalez-Rivera laughed. "Excellent deduction, Charles. So who do you think they really are?"

"I haven't the faintest idea, so why don't you tell me, sir?" Charles looked at Gonzalez-Rivera for a reaction, but the major's expression did not change. "You're still under suspicion for the murder. Could these men be a bunch of lawyers you brought over to clear you? Are you that worried?"

Gonzalez-Rivera merely patted Donnelly on the top of his helmet and said good-bye. At the same moment, St. John appeared beside the Jeep.

"Sorry I'm late, old boy. Got held up." He hopped into the driver's seat and started the engine.

Donnelly eyed St. John, envying his easy manner.

"Where's our driver?" Donnelly asked.

"Hell, man, we don't need a driver. I'm driving!"

Five miles down the road, their Jeep slowed to a stop. "That damned wire again," said John. He swore as he waved the trucks to pass him. Coleman stopped.

"What's up?" he asked. His voice was matter-of-fact, indicating he was not alarmed.

"Nothing, sir," replied John. "We'll catch up and pass you in a few minutes."

"Carry on, then," said Coleman as he waved them farewell.

Donnelly sat silently until the column pulled away, then he turned squarely to St. John and said, "I'm confused, Johnny."

"That sounds ominous. What are you talking about, Charles?"

"Johnny, my evidence points towards the barn. The girl was an allied agent, and she was supposed to meet you there."

St. John looked over at Donnelly. "Yes," he said sadly. "But how do you know that?"

Donnelly briefly explained about meeting Isabelle's friend. He was careful to leave out Marie's name.

"Please let me know what happened, Johnny. If anybody except me was in charge of this damned investigation, they'd have your skin nailed to the door and no questions asked. But I think I've got it figured out. Confirm it. Tell me."

St. John studied Charles for a long moment, then sighed. "Her name was Isabelle Foche. We had arranged to meet in the barn that morning. But I got delayed on the right flank. Remember, Coleman ordered me to go over to check Sauter's platoon? I was so damn late. Finally I made a quick stop at the C.P. to report to the colonel and was just heading to the barn when Buddy showed up with the news. Can you imagine how horrified I was when I heard there was a girl murdered with Ames? And when I saw her body... Charles, it was awful."

"I'd already figured it out exactly as you just told me. Johnny, you must have died."

Breathing deeply, St. John turned to Donnelly. "When I saw her like that, you're right. I wanted to die.

"We'd met a few times before." St. John paused and smiled sadly. "God, Charles, it was like magic. I loved her the moment I saw her."

Charles sighed; he knew all about that now. "Why didn't you report the whole thing to C.I.D.?"

"I did. They figured out right away that Ames was the rapist and somebody caught him at it and shot him. That's when they lost interest. But I made a report to Counter Intelligence, too. That's why they were swarming all over the place asking so many questions. Because of Isabelle, they're all stirred up about it, looking for leaks in our intelligence network, traitors in our units, tightening security all over the place. It's the old game of 'When in question, when in doubt, run in circles, scream and shout.' We know they're barking up the wrong tree, Charles. They're just as mystified as we are."

Charles thought for a moment. "I'm curious. What excuse did she give the Germans for being on their side of the Rhine?"

"Refugee from the German west bank of the Rhine, fleeing the awful Americans. She was from Alsace. She could easily pass for a German."

"Why didn't you tell all this to Coleman? Then, he'd have put you in charge of this damned investigation."

John smiled. "I'm not even supposed to tell you—or anybody else outside of intelligence. But you found out on your own.

"Charles, I didn't kill Ames. I wish I had when I had the chance, but I didn't, and I'll regret it until I die. My shooting Lou Ames at the minefield would have saved Isabelle's life. For a while, I felt like slitting my own throat as a gesture of atonement. I didn't want to live anymore."

"I'm sorry, Johnny."

"At least we know it was Ames who killed her."

Donnelly nodded. "And as soon as the ballistic reports come back, I'll be able to tell you who killed Ames and, more to the point, who hanged Buddy."

"You took the slugs to C.I.D.?"

"Yes, delivered them personally. I should have the results by next week if not sooner."

"Does Turner know that?"

Charles shrugged.

"You ought to have a bodyguard until then."

Charles laughed grimly, "I do. I've got you."

By now, they had the Jeep started again. They passed the small Task Force Coleman, as St. John studied his map, one hand still on the wheel.

"If I were you, I'd keep my eye on Gonzalez-Rivera, too," St. John said, as they crested a small hill. "I think I saw him going into your room one night."

"Well, damn him. Are you sure?"

"Looked like him."

They passed through the university town of Tubingen. Talking about Isabelle with Charles seemed to have cleared his mind and made him his old lighthearted self once more. Gradually the open fields gave way to hilly, wooded terrain. As the forest became denser, St. John slowed the Jeep.

"What are you doing?" asked Charles.

St. John smiled and stopped the Jeep. German troops poured out of the woods in front of them. John turned the Jeep around and sped back down the road. Charles heard rifles pop and bullets whistle past. He hunched down in his seat.

"Relax, Charles. Remember, I'm faster than a speeding bullet."

"Damn," said Donnelly. "You take these risks just to torment me, don't you?"

St. John just smiled. "Getting shot at by second-rate Jerry soldiers shouldn't bother you, tiger. After all, you're the hero of Belingen."

"Oh, shut the hell up."

Back at the convoy, St. John told Coleman there were enemy troops ahead of them, well-armed, and who appeared ready to fight. Coleman nodded and sent for the colonel in charge of the "strange squad," as it had come to be known. They were all middle-aged and self-assured. They did not act at all like the green replacements they were supposed to be. Replacements arrived young and died young. This group was "strange," indeed.

Coleman waited until he and the other colonel were out of earshot. "How important is it that we take this town quickly, Colonel?"

"Crucial."

"Can we delay a day or two?"

"Negative," the colonel answered, shaking his head sternly.

"We're close," said Coleman. "But if we fight our way through now, without artillery support or reinforcements, a lot of our men will be killed."

"We have no choice."

"Killed, Colonel. You still want that town at any cost?"

"Yes. At any cost."

Colonel Coleman conceived a plan of battle quickly. Paul Turner would take his company of infantry and verify whether or not there were SS troops approaching from behind and, if so, ambush them from the woods. The remaining infantry would move forward through the woods on either side of the road, flushing out the Germans until they fell back on their artillery support. Coleman, observing from a rise, would then call in air support to wipe out the Germans that had made it to the 88s. At the first air strike, a truck carrying Gonzalez-Rivera, the colonel and his "strange squad" would race for Hechingen, preceded by a truckful of infantry. The infantry would then secure the town quickly. Donnelly was to be in charge of the first truck. In case there was resistance at the town itself, he was to fight his way in.

"Charles," Coleman said, leading him away from the others. "Once you reach Hechingen, whatever Gonzalez-Rivera or that colonel says, goes. No questions asked. Do you understand?"

"Yes, sir."

The two trucks that were to make the dash to Hechingen stood bumper to bumper. Donnelly joined Colonel Coleman on a rise with his radio teams and staff.

The colonel pointed to the rear. "Look back there, Charles. Turner's doing his work well."

Donnelly saw smoke and heard weapons firing. German soldiers were sprawled all across the road. In the distance, he could see the landscape dotted with the tiny forms of retreating soldiers. In front of him, the firing in the woods grew louder. Coleman spoke into his radio and listened to the reply.

"We caught them by surprise," he said, with visible relief. "The bastards were watching the road, and our boys were on them before they knew what was happening." There was a crackling, and then an excited voice came through Coleman's radio.

"They're pulling out, running like hell," Coleman exclaimed, his voice triumphant. "Now, contact those Tactical Air Corps planes we have up there. Now. Now!" Coleman had set up the air strike before he sent in his infantry, and the planes awaited his command to begin their strafing and bombing runs.

The relief Charles felt was indescribable. Thank God for Colonel Coleman. He knew his beans, that was for sure. The roar of airplane engines drowned out his thoughts, as the planes thundered overhead, firing their machine guns and cannon, dropping their devastating bomb loads.

Donnelly heard the two truck motors turn over. He ran to the lead truck and pulled himself on board beside the driver just as it started to move.

Still under orders to get to Hechingen as fast as possible, the G.I. truck drivers spun around curves and sped over small hills, their tailgates falling open and crashing against the uneven terrain. Charles held on for dear life.

Then, thankfully, the town of Hechingen. He hoped it wasn't defended.

It perched on the side of a hill. The streets climbed, dropped and twisted through rows of picturesque little houses. In the distance, on a tree-clad mountain, stood a turreted castle straight out of a fairy tale. As they neared the edge of town, Charles raised his hand. "Hold it. Let the infantry secure the town on foot."

The trucks stopped, and Charles jumped down and organized his squad of infantry to enter the town, rifles at the ready. But Charles sensed there were no German troops about. White sheets hung from every window.

Gonzalez-Rivera jumped down from the second truck and dashed after Charles, followed closely by the colonel. "Nobody's to leave this town, do you hear me?" Gonzalez-Rivera shouted. "Secure all exits." His men jumped down and fanned out into the town. "We're expecting a unit of special Army engineers. Send them to me as soon as they arrive," Gonzalez-Rivera said to Charles.

As Charles said, "Yes, sir," and started walking away, a wiry, grey-haired squad member, now wearing major's insignia, trotted up to the colonel. "They're here. We found them. Heisenberg, Otto Hahn, the lot. And it looks like we're in time."

The three officers dashed off, leaving Charles standing alone in the middle of the street. As they disappeared, Charles heard the colonel say, "Use the secret code to contact Groves."

13

Things had happened so fast that Charles was surprised to see several trucks and Jeeps approaching the town. The rest of the Task Force Coleman wasn't expected to arrive for some time. They had to bring in their dispersed units, treat the wounded, provide for prisoners, collect the dead and make sure every man was accounted for. Charles stepped into the middle of the road and signaled the vehicles to stop.

A captain swung down from the lead truck. "Is this Hechingen?"

"Depends on who's asking," countered Donnelly.

"Special Engineer Force."

Charles recovered his memory and waved them through. He was tempted to crouch on the running board of one of the trucks and find out their destination, but he had other work to do. With his own two trucks safely secured beside some buildings, he went to see how successful the sergeant had been in sealing off the town. Two men stood at the end of each road leading in and out of it. They also checked every house for German troops, but they found only civilians in residence, and they seemed pitifully anxious to please the American soldiers. Hitler had led the German people to believe that the Americans were savages, who would slaughter them all. As the townspeople slowly realized they would not be hurt, they began to emerge from cellars and bomb shelters, blinking in the sunlight.

Charles was standing outside the Rathaus when the bürgermeister appeared.

The man cleared his throat nervously. *"Herr ubersturm fuhrer."* Clicking his heels together, he drew a piece of paper out of his pocket and read from it. "In the name of the council of Hechingen, I hereby surrender to you our town."

"I accept your capitulation in the name of the United States Army," Charles said.

The bürgermeister bowed formally, and scurried away.

After he left, Charles set about inspecting the town for suitable billets. He found a nice, clean house next to the Rathaus, and staked his claim on a room with a large feather bed, facing the street. Once the others arrived there would not be enough houses to go around, and many of the men would have to bivouac in the fields. Charles liked to be billeted close to headquarters, and he was sure Coleman would select the Rathaus as his C.P. Though its outside revealed only a solid structure, war-worn and undistinguished, the interior contained beautiful, high-beamed ceilings and coats of arms painted on the walls. Large porcelain stoves warmed the rooms, and the enormous reception hall would be perfect for the colonel's office.

Charles lay down on the big feather bed in his small room and closed his eyes. For a moment he was in Belingen, in Marie Dumont's little room. Where was she now? Perhaps she had left the hospital and returned to France. He hoped so. Charles had tried to get her out of his mind. Who knew if either of them would survive this war? And, if they did, would things be the same way between them? He was sure they would. She felt like a ghost in his life—so far away but always there.

Outside Charles heard a sound he could not remember hearing in a long time—children at play. He went to the bay window. Sure enough, three young girls were skipping rope below... and laughing. Charles sat down on the window seat and idly watched the town come back to life. With Hechingen secured, there was nothing left for him to do. Colonel Coleman wasn't due until tomorrow, and Charles had accomplished his mission. The mysterious "squad" had disappeared. What were they after? he wondered. If Hechingen was so vital to them, there was something important in it—something that Coleman had risked the lives of his men to get. What was here? Stolen masterpieces? A big shot from the Gestapo or SS in residence? Gold? Perhaps they were near a concentration camp, Charles thought, shuddering with disgust. He had heard of these terrible places, though, thus far, he had not yet come across any.

And what was Gonzalez-Rivera's role in the mission? Who was he, really? He claimed ignorance, yet he seemed suspiciously familiar with the members of the squad. Was he an intelligence agent using his position in the regiment as a cover? Perhaps Ames and Marks had found out something about his mission. Perhaps they had not been murdered, but assassinated... A hundred thoughts clouded Charles's mind.

He looked out the window just in time to see Gonzalez-Rivera climb into an engineer's Jeep and take off down the only road out of town, which looked like a continuation of the same road they came in on. Charles looked at his map. The road led directly to the next town, named Haigerloch, about twelve miles away. There the road ended. At least he knew where Gonzalez-Rivera was going.

Charles flagged down an engineer lieutenant's Jeep. "Going to Haigerloch?" he asked.

"Sure, hop in."

The two officers rode in silence. Charles figured the engineers and the "strange squad" were on some clandestine mission they didn't want to talk about, and he decided to be polite and not press it. The road wound through the hills until it came to the quaint little town of Haigerloch. Untouched by the war, its neat white houses with their red, blue or green windows made it look like a town of dollhouses. "You can leave me here," said Charles, at the outskirts.

"Not going to the cave?" asked the lieutenant.

"Not yet," replied Charles. "Thanks for the ride."

His eyes followed the Jeep as far as they could. Then Charles began to walk in that direction. It took him an hour before he saw the olive-drab vehicles parked on a side street opposite what looked like a rock wall. A square entrance was cut into the rock face. Charles approached the entrance cautiously. A chair stood outside the entrance, but if a sentry had been posted, he was nowhere in sight. A battered sign above the door signified it as a beer storage cellar.

The door was slightly ajar. Hesitantly, Charles entered a hallway, lit by the glow of a nearby generator. Beyond, he saw a large stone cellar about forty feet deep. In the middle of it was a cylindrical hole about twelve feet in diameter into which something had been sunk. Gonzalez-Rivera, the colonel and their companions were talking animatedly with a group of middle-aged German civilians, over piles of paper containing notes of some kind. He heard one of the civilians say to the colonel in a low voice, "Tell me, *Herr* Doctor, my colleagues believe your people have already achieved a nuclear reaction. Is so?"

"I'm not at liberty to answer that," the colonel replied curtly.

Charles thought, my God, all these men are scientists, but what the hell is a nuclear reaction?

At that moment lights came on above him. He froze.

Gonzalez-Rivera stopped talking to one of the Germans when he saw Charles. "What are you doing here, Donnelly?"

Ignoring Gonzalez-Rivera, Charles spoke to the colonel. "Sir, is there anything I can do for you here?"

"Yes, Captain. Thank you very much. You can post more efficient guards at the entrance to keep out the curious, if you will."

"Yes, sir," Charles stammered.

Gonzalez-Rivera followed Charles outside and pulled him aside. "Will you tell me what the hell you're doing here, Donnelly?"

Charles looked Ramon in the eye. "Tell me, *Herr* Doctor, is it true you've already achieved a nuclear reaction?"

Gonzalez-Rivera grabbed Donnelly's arm and silently guided him away from the street into a path between two houses. "Now." he demanded. "Tell me what you know."

"I know you're working on a nuclear reaction project, and I know it's very important."

"That's all?"

"Yes, that's it."

"But you don't know why it's important, do you?" said Gonzalez-Rivera.

Charles shook his head.

"I could probably have you court-martialed and put away in solitary for the duration, and maybe I should," said Ramon, his eyes narrowing to slits.

"Who are you?" Charles asked.

"I'm a physicist. And an engineer," he said with more than a hint of arrogance. "And I also design weapons for the War Department."

"So you're not a spy."

"Hardly," the major said with a disdainful laugh. "I was sent over here to see how my equipment was holding up in actual combat. Then this mission came along. And now you've stumbled right into it. You're a true pain in the ass, Donnelly."

"What exactly is your mission?" Charles pressed.

"I can't tell you that."

"Look, Ramon, I risked my life for whatever's in that cave. So did the rest of the men."

"What's in that cave is worth more than any of your lives," Gonzalez-Rivera said coldly.

"Then I'm sure the information I have will be worth a lot to someone," Charles said. The major was a prick and he was damned if he'd be intimidated by him.

"You wouldn't dare." Gonzalez-Rivera gripped his arm so tightly Charles could feel his hand prickle.

"Try me," Charles's voice was cold.

Gonzalez-Rivera went silent, undecided. "Swear on your word of honor as an officer and a gentleman and by everything you hold most holy, that you won't reveal anything you've heard today to a soul."

"I swear it."

"All right." Gonzalez-Rivera took a deep breath. "As you probably know, splitting the nucleus of an atom will release tremendous energy. If it's done right, the neutrons and protons produced by the original fission will strike and split the surrounding nuclei, culminating in a chain reaction and generating an unbelievable amount of energy and power. So, achieving a nuclear chain reaction will make possible a device so destructive it will make all other weapons of war look like children's toys. Such a weapon could mean the difference between winning or losing this war.

"A few months ago we received some shocking news," Gonzalez-Rivera continued. "Our intelligence service confirmed to us that the Nazis were still working on a similar project. We thought they had abandoned it, but our information was wrong. So, now we had to find out how close they were to developing a nuclear capability. Even more important, we had to capture their atomic scientists with all their notes and equipment before they fell into the wrong hands. Our sources indicated that the center of Nazi research and experimentation was Hechingen. Because of Allied bombing raids on Berlin, the Nazis moved the Kaiser Wilhelm Institute from Berlin to Hechingen, but the actual experiments are not done there. That's a nuclear test reactor they have in the cave here at Haigerloch. They have heavy water and uranium—the works. And it hasn't been destroyed or captured. It's still intact and was in German hands."

"In other words, they would have been able to achieve this nuclear reaction, if we hadn't gotten here in time to stop them?" asked Charles.

Gonzalez-Rivera nodded. "Yes, but not soon. Not before the war ended. You see, Hitler's support for the project is less than wholehearted, and he's been stingy about funding it. He and his scientists were mostly interested in developing a nuclear engine for submarines. That's why our colonel is so happy. We've ascertained exactly how much progress the Nazis have made. They were on the right track, but they're still far behind us." As he spoke, the major's voice changed, becoming excited with the subject. Charles actually liked him by the time he had finished his explanation.

"Why didn't they concentrate all their resources and efforts on this super-destructive weapon?"

"Because Hitler and the other top Nazis thought of nuclear physicists as Jews, since mostly Jewish scientists had been involved in it. So, they missed the strategic importance of developing an atomic weapon." He paused for a breath, then finished, "So that's it, Donnelly. You know everything. And, thanks to this mission, so do we. Not knowing how far the Nazis had gotten would have been unthinkable."

"I have just one more question," Charles said.

Gonzalez-Rivera raised one eyebrow. "Don't push it, Donnelly."

"What were you doing in my room last week?"

"You know about that?" Gonzalez-Rivera said, genuinely surprised. "You must be a better detective than I gave you credit for."

"So you admit it."

"I do. Your investigation was making me suspicious. All your questions might have been a cover for spying on me and my work."

"Me, a spy?"

Gonzalez-Rivera laughed. "After you came to my room to drag me to the toolshed, I discovered that one of my documents was missing. I had to be sure you hadn't taken it. Later, I found it under the bed." Gonzalez-Rivera looked at his watch. "I have to get back to work. See you around."

"Yeah, see you."

Charles thought about everything Ramon had said. If Gonzalez-Rivera was telling him the truth, the race to Hechingen was one of the single most important missions of the war. It was ironic; Hitler had spent so much time looking for a secret weapon, yet because of his prejudice against the Jews, he had missed developing the most supreme weapon of them all, the one that could have won the war for him.

The sun was settled over the low hills surrounding Hechingen. Sitting with the wind in his face, Charles gazed out at the peaceful countryside around him. The war would soon be over, and he hoped it wouldn't be long before this country recovered from the evil that had insidiously, but briefly, entered its soul.

Roaring engines and marching feet awoke Charles the next morning. The task force had arrived. Quickly he threw on his uniform and ran downstairs to greet the colonel. Within minutes, Coleman's Jeep came roaring down the street carrying the colonel and three of his officers. Charles waved him down.

"Ah, Donnelly, good." Coleman jumped out. "I gather from the guards you posted that the town has been secured. Where are Gonzalez-Rivera and his men?"

Charles hesitated. He had promised the major that he would keep secret all that he had learned. But if Coleman went to Haigerloch he would surely discover the cave for himself. "They aren't here, sir. I think they went to another town somewhere."

At that moment Gonzalez-Rivera appeared beside him. "Colonel Coleman. Sir." Gonzalez-Rivera stood at attention.

"At ease, Major. What news?" Coleman asked.

"The squad has completed its mission. The men will make their own way back to London under the colonel's command, sir."

"And I assume that you can now tell me the nature of that mission?"

"Negative, sir. The men went on ahead. I was not included in their party."

"But Donnelly just said you were with them."

"Captain Donnelly didn't know I was here, readying the Command Post for you, sir." He gestured to the Rathaus. "I think you'll find everything in order."

Coleman looked at him suspiciously, then followed him into the C.P. Charles fell in behind and waited quietly by the door.

Inside, Colonel Coleman settled himself in a large velvet chair under a high, latticed window. "Sit down, Major," he instructed, and Gonzalez-Rivera pulled up a chair beside him. "I received orders yesterday from Washington. You are to be sent back to the States. Effective tomorrow afternoon. You'll be going via London."

"Thank you, sir."

"Interesting timing, considering that you know nothing about the squad or its mission, don't you think?"

Gonzalez-Rivera shrugged. "Just got lucky, I guess."

Coleman leaned forward purposefully. "You'll be accompanying the colonel."

The major examined a spot of mud on his trousers. "Will that be all, sir?"

Coleman looked up at the timbered ceiling. "Dismissed."

"Arrogant son of a bitch," Coleman said under his breath, as Gonzalez-Rivera left the room. "Donnelly," he shouted, "stop skulking in that corner and get over here." Charles emerged from the shadows and sat down in the seat vacated by the major. "I'd like to nail that guy, Charles. He may be competent, but he thinks he's above the law. I hate that."

"I understand, sir."

"Which reminds me; when do those bullets come back?"

"Any time now."

"Hope they don't get lost in the shuffle. We'll be moving on again, soon. Maybe a day or two. We're getting distressing reports from the front. In the forward regiments almost every rifle company is experiencing fire fights, and their rate of advance is slowing considerably. Entire Jerry units are hiding in the woods so they can ambush one of our Jeeps or trucks. Most of them just want to escape." Coleman sighed. "It's the men we lose now that break my heart. A few more weeks and it will all be over. It's just mopping up from here on in."

Coleman walked to the open fire and rubbed his hands together. The April air was still cool and damp from the morning dew. Facing the fire, Coleman said, "I've been offered command of the Fifteenth Infantry Division, Charles. I've decided to take it."

"Congratulations, sir. You'll make a wonderful major general."

"I hope my command will be over so quickly that I won't have the chance to prove myself."

"We'll miss you, sir."

There was a brisk knock on the door, and Paul Turner charged in and asked abruptly, "Where should I put my men, sir?"

"Donnelly, why don't you show Turner where to go."

"I'd like to," Charles muttered under his breath. Then, begrudgingly, he accompanied Turner into the dimly-lit foyer.

"After you," Turner said, as the door shut behind them.

"No, after you."

"Nervous, Charlie? Scared you're gonna get it in the back? Don't worry. I wouldn't do it here. The colonel might not like it."

"I'd prefer not to take that risk."

"Suit yourself." Turner shoved past Charles and walked out onto the street. "I'm sure you don't want to end up stuck like a pig in the woods, huh?"

"Your billet is in here," Charles said, doing his best to ignore Turner's taunts. He opened the door to the house.

"I think I'll get my men settled first; I'll come find you later tonight." He smiled menacingly, revealing a set of stained, uneven teeth. "Don't wait up."

Though bright sunshine warmed the quiet street, Charles shivered with a sense of foreboding.

But as he watched Turner strut off, Charles felt his fear evaporate, replaced by icy anger. He was not going to wait for Paul

Turner to come after him. If Turner wanted a real showdown, he would have to face it now, in the open, in broad daylight.

"Hold it!"

Turner stopped.

"You want to knock me off, too? Well, do it now or I'll gun you down where you stand."

Turner laughed. "And justice will be served, huh?"

"Just tell me one thing, Turner. I understand why you killed Ames, but why Marks?"

"Piss off, Donnelly. Buddy was my friend. He saved my ass more than once with the colonel. I didn't kill him. Or that little shit Lou Ames, either."

"You expect me to believe that?"

"You're a fool, Donnelly. A blind, bigoted fool. You think just because I ain't got a fancy degree from some stupid college I'd kill my friend? Why don't you try shaking down one of your elegant friends like Cary Grant over there." He waved to St. John who was at the other end of the street heading towards them.

"Johnny didn't kill Ames."

"And how do you know that?"

Donnelly hesitated. "He told me."

Turner laughed. "Well, that's first-class detective work, Sherlock."

"Shut up, Turner, and tell me what you know."

"All I know is that Johnny and Ames played a lot of cards, and Johnny kept losing—owed Ames a lot of money. Well, your nice Mr. Johnny St. John may talk good, but he ain't got a penny to his fancy little name. Poor as a church mouse, he is. Just like me. And maybe spoiled rich kid Ames was cheating. But Johnny woulda had to pay him or lose his commission, lose everything he'd fought for in his life. You think about it, detective. You think about it good and hard next time you and Blue Eyes are out in the deep dark woods looking for Krauts. You might find a bullet in your back instead."

Charles's mind raced. Johnny had said something about a poker game, it was true.

"Afternoon, gentlemen," St. John said as he neared. "I've been looking for you everywhere, Charles. Two of the headquarters' Jeeps never showed up. Coleman wants us to go look for them."

"Have a nice drive," Turner said, grinning at Charles. "If I don't see you later, it's been swell." With that he was gone.

"He pestering you again?" St. John asked.

Charles nodded distractedly. "What was that about a Jeep?"

"Two Jeeps. Never showed. Coleman's afraid they got ambushed. Let's go."

Charles followed St. John to the Jeep. "When were they last seen?"

"In the woods outside of town."

"The woods?"

"Yes. What's going on, Charles? You seem a bit preoccupied."

"Nothing. Sorry." Charles climbed into the Jeep.

They drove out of town on a dirt road lined with leafy trees. This was the approach that the last of Coleman's task force had taken. They had gone a few miles when Charles noticed a group of small, broken pine trees on an incline just off the main road. Some larger pines had white gashes where their bark had been scraped off. Only something rugged and fast-moving could have done such damage. He laid his hand on Johnny's arm. "Slow down." Charles pointed to the trees. "Something went down there."

St. John stopped the Jeep and the two officers got out. Their eyes followed the path cut through the young pines. Both men spotted two Jeeps lying halfway down the incline. A line of thick pines had broken their descent, smashing the front of one Jeep, overturning the other. Charles and St. John went down the hill slowly, grabbing onto branches for balance and support. They found no one in the first vehicle, but Johnny pointed beyond it. Following his direction, Charles saw two bodies that had evidently been flung from the Jeep when it hit the trees. Charles started to go down to them but John grabbed his arm. "Let Graves Registration take care of it."

"Suppose they're alive. We can't take a chance on leaving them without checking."

St. John conceded and together they headed down the hill. When they reached the second Jeep, there was no doubt—the soldiers trapped underneath had been dead for hours. John bent to examine the bodies more closely. "They've been shot." He made his way over to the other two bodies. "All of them. Peppered with small caliber bullets. Must've been a Kraut ambush. They were probably after the Jeeps, but our guys made sure they didn't get—"

He stopped, rising slowly, an odd expression on his face. "Don't move," he instructed Charles. Then, with quiet deliberation, he drew his pistol and took a bead on Donnelly. Paralyzed to the spot, Charles felt tiny beads of cold sweat break out across his forehead.

"Johnny, I—"

"Quiet," St. John hissed, as he put a round in the chamber as quietly as possible.

Charles closed his eyes as St. John pulled the trigger. He heard a deafening bang, then another and another and another, until the clip was empty. Finally Charles was aware of nothing but the smell of gunsmoke in the empty woods. He opened one eye.

"Got them," St. John said, putting a full clip into his .45.

Charles turned. Behind him, at the bottom of the incline, two German soldiers lay dead, their guns still aimed at his back.

"What's the matter, Charles? You look like you've seen a ghost," St. John said.

"It's... I..." Donnelly was stunned at the ease with which St. John could raise his gun and fire at men. It's like he's killing flies, he thought. And though he shot eight times, to hit each man even once at that range with a .45 was damned good shooting.

"Stop your stammering and let's get back to headquarters. I'm starving. Maybe we can get Montana to cook up one of his blue-plate specials."

14

Charles stared at the hands of the mahogany grandfather clock in his temporary office. It had been a long, wearying day. Since Charles and St. John had found the two Jeeps the day before, Donnelly had been trying to concentrate on the murder of Buddy Marks. He wasn't concerned about Lou Ames anymore. Ames deserved what he got. He had raped and killed the girl, Isabelle. Somebody caught him in the act and executed him on the spot. Marks showed up. Whoever shot Ames was a friend of Marks's and convinced him to keep his mouth shut—either that, or they both concocted the story of an enlisted man committing the murder and running away. But why not just tell the truth? Fear of Coleman's reaction? Perhaps. At least that's logical. Otherwise, he was protecting somebody, but who would Buddy Marks protect to that extent? Turner, certainly. But Charles doubted that Turner would have hanged Marks that way. He genuinely liked Buddy. How about St. John? Marks admired and almost worshipped Johnny. John would certainly have shot Ames if he'd caught him raping Isabelle. But would John have hanged Marks? No.

There was a knock on the door, and Montana entered.

"Sorry to interrupt, sir, but this letter just came for you and it looks important." He placed an envelope red-marked CONFIDENTIAL on Donnelly's desk. The back flap of the envelope bore the special stamp of the Criminal Investigation Department.

Charles's heart beat faster. He could almost hear it pounding in his chest. In a moment, he was going to know for a certainty who shot Ames and hanged Buddy Marks. He ripped the envelope open. He read the results of the ballistics tests: A– Negative. B– Negative. C– Negative. D– Negative. E– Negative. The note at the bottom of the report said, "As you can see, our forensic comparisons indicate that none of the submitted bullets match the sample sent us."

Charles sat very still. There were only five officers who carried .45 caliber pistols at the Rhine; Ames was shot by a .45, yet none of the sample slugs matched the one Charles had dug out of the barn wall.

"Are you okay, sir?" asked Montana.

Charles jumped even though he was sitting down. "I didn't know you were still here," he said.

"Thought I'd stick around to see if you'd need any help picking up the bad guy," said Montana. "It don't take no genius to figure out what was in that envelope, sir. You gonna tell me now or wait until you got him?"

Without answering, Charles handed Montana the report.

"How can that be, sir?" asked Montana.

Charles shook his head slowly. "You tell me and we'll both know," he said hesitantly.

Both men sat silent for another fifteen minutes.

Montana spoke first. "Somebody turned in his .45 and drew another," he said.

"How's that?" asked Charles.

"Well, sir, the supply sergeant keeps everything he can lay his hands on so he can have stuff available in a pinch. In Normandy, I got my carbine shot right out of my hands by a sniper. Took a big chunk out of the stock, so it broke in half. I went to the supply sergeant for another. But then I got this brainstorm. I asked him if he could issue me a .45 seeing as how I'm a driver and a carbine ain't much good, nohow, and he says, 'sure', and I drew this here pistol."

Charles hadn't paid much attention to what arms Montana carried, but now he remembered that he always had a holstered .45 attached to his web belt. Charles stood up. "Let's go see the supply sergeant," he said.

The supply sergeant was a man named Cooper, who was by turns taciturn or jolly. He was almost like a child, except that he was six feet tall and was rotund and red-faced with thinning blond hair. He had set up his supply room in what looked like a small former schoolhouse.

Donnelly did not waste time. "Did any officer for any reason turn in his .45 after the Rhine crossing?"

"Yes, sir," replied the sergeant.

"Who?" asked Charles, since it was clear that Sergeant Cooper was not going to elaborate.

"Well," said Cooper, "Captain Turner did. The firing pin was broke and the housing was sliding funny like. Sort of off-kilter."

Charles thought, Turner. Of course! No wonder he changed his mind and didn't give a damn about the ballistics tests.

"Did you replace the pistol?"

"Yes, sir. We had a captain was hit bad last fall. I got his pistol back from the aid station. I heard he died later of his wounds in the hospital."

"You gave his pistol to Captain Turner?"

"Yes, sir. But we got a man here who used to be in ordnance and can fix most anything. Didn't take him long, neither, till that pistol was as good as new."

That was enough for Donnelly. The pistol Turner used for the test was not the one he carried during the Rhine crossing. That would explain the results of the test—and would convict Paul Turner just as sure as hell. Now he had the murderer. Now he could avenge Buddy Marks. We'll keep the pistol and hang Paul Turner. And Buddy? Marks trusted Turner. It would have been easy. But why? Buddy must have seen Turner at the barn. Then it would be: to Hell with Marks. I have to cover my own ass. Anyway, murder solved. Now just wrap it up.

All he had to do was make sure the pistol Turner carried at the Rhine was kept in safe keeping until the court-martial. He turned to the supply sergeant. "I assume you still have Captain Turner's pistol."

"Uh, no, sir," said Sergeant Cooper.

"What?" said Charles, "Why not?"

"It's a long story, sir."

"I have time, Sergeant."

"Well, sir, the colonel had some trouble with his, so I exchanged it for Captain Turner's."

"The colonel?"

"Yes, sir." The sergeant sounded tentative. "He told me not to tell. Said it would look funny for the commander of the regiment to get his pistol all fouled up like that. So please don't let him know I told you."

Donnelly smiled at the sergeant to put him at ease. "Don't worry," he said. "Remember, I work for him too. But tell me, what was wrong with his .45?"

"He was cleaning it and the spring flew out. Often does."

Charles nodded. Clearly he'd had the same experience a few times, as had many new officers, but he had always recovered the spring.

"Only the colonel couldn't find the spring. The kind of dumb thing a recruit would pull," said the sergeant, feeling more comfortable now with Donnelly. "We could have found another spring for him right here, but he wanted another pistol. Said he couldn't trust his no more."

Charles nodded. "So you gave him Captain Turner's to replace his."

The sergeant said, "Yeah. I gave him Captain Turner's."

Charles took a deep breath before he spoke. "Did the colonel know it was formerly Captain Turner's pistol?"

"Sure. I told him, sir. We went out in the woods and fired two full clips so the colonel could get the feel of the .45 and be sure it was okay and all."

"Thank you very much, Sergeant Cooper. You've been a great help to me. But if the colonel told you not to tell anybody about his changing pistols, how come you told me without an argument?"

The sergeant scratched his head. "Well, sir, the colonel wasn't very nice about it. Sort of as if he was threatening me or something. Can't explain it, but it upset me and made me mad."

Charles said very slowly, "Sergeant, please do me a favor. Keep the colonel's old .45 in a very safe place and don't let it out until I come to get it. Okay?"

"Yes, sir. I got me a field safe just like the colonel's. I'll keep it there."

Montana had stayed out of the exchanges between Sergeant Cooper and Captain Donnelly on purpose. He knew Donnelly didn't want to be interrupted during his conversation with the supply sergeant. Now he said, "I guess I was right, wasn't I, sir? But I still don't know who shot Ames and hanged Lieutenant Marks."

"You did good, Montana. Now I need time to think."

Charles walked slowly on his way back to headquarters. Since Coleman didn't object to the ballistics test, even volunteered to participate, it means he *knew* that Turner did not shoot Ames or hang Marks. But if Paul didn't, who did? In his heart of hearts, Charles knew there was only one answer.

15

Charles entered the headquarters and went straight to the clerk on duty.

"Where's the colonel?" he asked the clerk.

"He told me that, if you came looking for him, to try the castle up on the hill, sir. The old man was going to see about commandeering it as field comm—"

Charles was already gone.

The castle was a rococo frivolity, built by one of the many mad princes who once ruled the hinterlands of Germany. Its towering turrets and stark battlements hung over the battered and muddy old town like a picture from Grimm. Charles walked through the portcullis feeling as if he was stepping into the jaws of some dreadful monster.

The vast entrance hall sat empty, abandoned. The fine old masonry, damp and crumbling, held once-rich tapestries, now in tatters, like the ragged clothes of a defeated king.

Charles found himself reluctant to raise his voice; it seemed sacrilegious in the funereal atmosphere of the old schloss. Forcing himself, he called, "Colonel Coleman," and listened to his voice echo through the empty vastness.

Finally, on his third try, Coleman answered and Charles climbed the grand staircase, following the sound of the colonel's voice. He found Coleman in an empty banquet hall. He imagined

Teutonic knights feasting in such a room, their harsh voices raised in celebration of some bloody victory. Colonel Coleman, pacing the flagstone floor in his drab, woolen, olive-green uniform and old field jacket, looked small and out of place in such surroundings, and for the first time Charles saw that his superior officer—the soldier he respected and admired, a skilled fighter and leader of men—was also a vulnerable, tired man.

"Charles, welcome. How do you like our new headquarters? Quite baronial, isn't it?" Coleman laughed.

Charles saluted formally and stood at attention. "Sir, I have the results of the ballistics tests."

Coleman stopped his pacing.

"Ah, good. And what do they tell you?"

"According to the tests, the bullet that killed Ames was not fired from any of our pistols."

Coleman did not look surprised. "I never did put much faith in ballistics tests."

"Besides, you were armed with Turner's .45," said Charles.

"How do you know that?"

"Sergeant Cooper told me."

"So?" said the colonel.

"So you knew that Turner didn't shoot Lou Ames, which means you know who did. And whoever did the deed was very careful to cover his tracks. It's doubtful he'd confide in anybody. The only conclusion is, sir, that you shot your nephew."

"Nonsense!"

Charles shook his head sadly. "I'll tell you what happened, Colonel. You found your nephew doing this terrible thing, and you cracked. The dishonor is unbearable. The only way to avoid it is to shoot Ames dead and later say he was shot by the rapist and died a hero."

Coleman raised his hand and opened his mouth, but Charles stopped him by cutting the air with his right hand.

"Then, along comes Buddy," he continued. "You know he'll do anything for you. You make him a co-conspirator—until you can conveniently eliminate him, which you did as soon as I started to question him hard. *That* is what makes you a monster, Colonel Coleman. That I can never forgive. You could have gotten away with killing Ames. He was no good and you caught him in the act. I don't think that, even if I'd been competent enough to figure it out, I'd have turned you in. I'd have let you get away with the lie that Ames caught somebody else and paid with his life. But Buddy Marks trusted you and would have done anything for you. And you killed him in cold blood. I can't prove that in court, but I sure as hell do have the ballistics evidence to get you hanged for shooting Lou Ames, just as sure as God made green apples. I have the pistol you carried at the Rhine.

"I'd ask to see your belt, but I'm sure you discarded it the very day I mentioned that Ames had yanked off the killer's clip pouch."

"You're speculating, Charles. No more. No less."

Charles waited and watched as the colonel's expression dissolved into a mask of tired resignation. "It's funny, isn't it?" said Coleman. "The whole thing, the whole damned thing comes down to the ballistics tests on five .45 slugs—and your lack of compassion."

"St. John actually gave me the clue, sir. He said to me once, 'If any of us caught Ames raping the girl, we wouldn't shoot him. We'd turn him over to be court-martialed and hanged.' Then I realized that you were a suspect, too. So there was one, only one, person who would not do that but would have shot Ames to save the family from disgrace, and that person was you, sir."

The two men stood silently for a moment.

"You know, Donnelly, I never dreamed you'd survive Belingen." Coleman laughed. "Yes, the Uriah tactic, as you call it. If you'd gotten knocked off, I could have tossed away the damned bullets and everybody would have forgotten the whole thing. It would have worked, too, if it hadn't been for Johnny, damn his hide! All our artillery had strict instructions to carry out fire missions only on the main objective under penalty of court-martial. Without artillery, you'd have been gone for sure."

"I see," Charles said soberly. "You wanted the Germans to do your dirty work for you."

Coleman nodded. "It would have simplified everything."

"Johnny didn't bother with division artillery. He knew the orders. He went straight to corps and got Long Toms onto Belingen."

"The son of a bitch! But no use crying about it. Well done, Donnelly. You've done a good job, and you'll be getting the Medal of Honor for capturing those damned SS generals. Strange how things work out." He paced up and down the room, drifting into deep thought.

Charles asked, "Why did you do it, Colonel?" He'd already told Coleman, now he wanted Coleman to tell him.

The Colonel looked up with surprise. "Why? You have to ask why? That bastard, that monster.... My father was a soldier. My father's father was a soldier. The name 'Coleman' has been known and respected in Virginia for over two hundred and fifty years. And that animal, my sister's only son.... My God, I saw him cut that poor girl's throat. The blood—"

"Isabelle," said Charles faintly.

Coleman looked up. "What?"

"The girl, sir. Her name was Isabelle."

"Well, whoever she was, I'm damned sorry for her."

"Yes, sir. So am I."

Coleman put his hands to his temples but said nothing.

"Please sir, go on. I'd like to hear what happened."

Coleman breathed slowly. "I was out trying to get a better view of the battle when I heard screams. They were coming from the barn. I looked through the slats in the barn wall and saw a G.I. raping a girl. I threw open the door and pointed my .45 at the man. He leapt to his feet and, my God, it was Lou. I couldn't move. Do you know what he did when he saw me? He laughed. He just laughed at me. Said he'd done it before. Asked me if I wanted her next. I told him to stop, told him she would tell the authorities, that he had dishonored the family name. We're decent people. Respected! Do you hear me? Respected. But he just laughed, said it was no problem, but if I was worried about it... and then he slit her throat. That poor girl. I had to kill him, Charles. I had to. Who would have done anything differently?" Coleman paused. "Would you?"

Then, he seemed to remember something. "I'd have gotten away with it, too, except for one thing: my first shot missed. Those damned .45s—they can't hit a target three feet away. Lou left the girl lying dead and came at me, grabbed my belt. I believe he meant to knife me as he had that poor girl. But I fired again, so fast and close-up I hit him right in the chest, right through his heart."

Charles shook his head slowly. "And Buddy?" he asked sadly.

"Yes. Poor Marks." Coleman seemed mesmerized, as if he were re-living the scene. "He showed up just after I did it. Said he'd heard a scream."

"'So did I,' I told him. 'And this is what I found—Ames raping this poor girl. He slashed her throat, Buddy. So I had to shoot him. That's exactly what you would have done, too.'

"'Yes, sir, it is,' he said.

"'So we're in this together,' I told him. 'Let's get our story straight. You will say you arrived before Lou died. With his last breath, he told you that an enlisted man shot him when he caught the man raping the girl. Then, you will say you dashed out and saw a sergeant running away with a smoking M-1. Got it?'

"Well, Charles, you know Buddy. He just nodded and said 'Yes, sir.' The boy would have done anything for me, as you say. So I told him to go bury Ames's knife in the woods." He seemed reluctant to do that, so, since he was standing inside the barn with me, I slammed him up against the wall. I suppose that's when he tore his jacket. 'We're in this together, Buddy!' I said again. 'Our stories have to be the same, and you have to bury that knife!' He did, of course, but only half-heartedly. That's why you were able to find it so easily.

"Why he said he never entered the barn baffles me. I guess he made it up, trying to be clever. When you found that piece of cloth, it worked to his detriment and my benefit. It made it so much easier to make him out a liar, and therefore, a murderer."

Charles nodded. None of this surprised him much. "Then, you realized Buddy would crack under intense interrogation."

Coleman nodded. "He would have. I had to silence him. I asked him to meet me on the other side of town with the rope I'd told him to draw from supply in your name. When he got there, I asked him to inspect the tires on the Jeep and while he was leaning over, his helmet fell off. His helmet was always falling off. Right then, I whacked him on the back of the head with the wrench I was holding. That's when I killed him, I'm pretty sure. But by hanging him from the tree, I thought it would look like he had executed himself for his crime. When I hanged him from the tree in that orchard, it never occurred to me that it had rained there and the ground was muddy. I was too excited, too scared I suppose. But I shouldn't have overlooked something like that. You were very clever to notice it, Charles."

Donnelly shook his head.

The colonel stopped for a moment and examined a large canvas depicting some ancient battle scene in all its heraldic grandeur. "I switched pistols as soon as you told me you were returning to the barn. I realized you might find the slug from my first shot, so I switched just in case you might take ballistics tests, which you did. Once you start killing, it's hard to stop. I thought it would end with Lou. But you lose yourself, Donnelly. You stop caring. To tell you the truth, it wasn't that hard to kill Buddy."

The colonel turned around slowly, his pistol pointed at Donnelly. "Now please put your piece on the ground, Captain."

Donnelly stood for a moment, startled. Somehow, in all the excitement of discovery, he had never once considered the obvious—that now Coleman would have to murder him, as well. Charles drew his pistol and dropped it to the floor.

"You gain nothing by killing me, sir."

"By not killing you," Coleman said sternly, "I lose every-thing. There are armies to command, a war to be won. I am Colonel Lawrence Lightfoot Coleman. I have a duty to my country. Why do you think I drew you up here alone? I knew the C.I.D. report had arrived. I knew you'd want to see me right away. So, I've been waiting for you—here, with no witnesses."

"You're insane, sir. You need help."

Coleman picked up Donnelly's pistol, stuck it in his belt and pushed Charles towards a spiral staircase that seemed to wind up indefinitely. "Start climbing, Captain!"

Their footsteps echoed on the stone stairs, as they climbed the tower until finally reaching a low doorway. Both men were short of breath. "Open it!" Coleman said tersely.

Charles stepped outside. They stood high up on a parapet of the north tower. Through the battlements Charles could see deep lavender clouds scudding across a blood-red sky, as the sun sank low on the horizon.

"If you shoot me, they'll know."

"Yes, Charles. I'm aware of that. That's why I'm going to ask you to jump. They'll say you did the honorable thing."

"I'm afraid I can't do that, sir. You can keep killing if you like, but I won't jump. You'll have to shoot me and take the consequences yourself. After all the practice, I should think it would be quite easy." Charles stood tall and prepared to take the bullet.

Colonel Coleman hesitated. For a moment it looked as though he might put his gun away. "You're a good man, Charles. I'm sorry it had to end this way. I suppose I'll have to fire a couple of shots from your pistol to prove I acted in self-defense." He raised his .45 and aimed it directly at Charles's heart.

"Drop it, sir!" A voice rang out from the stairwell. Paul Turner stepped out of the shadows, his Tommy gun pointed at Coleman. When Coleman didn't respond, Turner sprayed the wall behind the colonel with a barrage of bullets. "I said, 'Drop it!'"

Astonished, Coleman let his pistol fall to the ground.

"Your nephew was a pig, Colonel, but Buddy was my friend. It ain't right, what you did, Colonel. It just ain't right." Turner picked up Coleman's .45 and threw it to Donnelly. "Sorry, Sherlock. I was following you; thought you was the killer. Guess I was after the wrong man."

Donnelly breathed, hardly able to talk. "I'm glad, Paul. You're a good man. You saved my life."

Together they turned to Coleman. Turner said, "We're takin' you in, sir."

"Yes..." Coleman said, dazed. "Yes, of course. It is your duty. Thank you, Paul."

"Come on, Colonel," Charles added gently.

Coleman shook his head as if to clear it. "Could I just have one minute alone, before you bring me in?"

Turner looked at Charles for confirmation, then said, "Yeah, that'd be okay."

The two officers stepped into the stairwell and closed the door, allowing their colonel his final moment of dignity.

Donnelly reached into his field jacket for his usual chocolate bar and offered half of it to Paul Turner as they waited in the darkness. Turner accepted and ate his half in huge bites.

Donnelly was glad he couldn't see Turner's face. He took a small bite of chocolate, his appetite gone. He heard the muffled scream that died away almost instantly.

"Better get back," he said.

"Yeah. He must have fell," said Paul Turner.

"Now he belongs to the Graves Registration crew," commented Charles.

16

Charles Donnelly and John St. John sat in a beer garden relaxing after the strain of having to give testimony at the short hearing into Colonel Coleman's death, which found that the colonel was overly tired and fell from the castle's rampart.

Charles broke the silence. "There were two things that I could never understand: Why had the killer bothered to hide Ames's knife, and why Ames hadn't drawn his gun. He must have heard his killer coming in—that barn door creaked so loudly you could hear it in Berlin.

"Coleman was the only one Ames didn't fear. That's why Ames didn't draw his gun. That's why his face had an expression of surprise in death—not because he'd been caught with his pants down, but because his uncle had actually shot him." Charles finished his beer.

"Then, the event that finally clinched it in my mind later was the realization that Coleman sent me into Belingen on a suicide mission with a handful of men to take on five hundred crack SS storm troopers. He wanted me dead. At first, I think one of the reasons Coleman appointed me to investigate was because he knew damned well I didn't have any experience in that kind of work. He figured he'd picked a dummy, and that I'd soon get tired of it and give up. When he realized he'd picked the wrong man, he had to get rid of me, somehow."

"What I don't understand," said John, "is why Coleman was so insistent on searching for the killer. If he'd have been smart, he'd have let it drop, just like the C.I.D. did."

Donnelly shook his head slowly. "No, Johnny. He had to take that attitude. Ames was his nephew, remember? How would it have looked if he'd simply said, 'Ho hum. Somebody murdered my nephew, but let's forget about it and get on with the war.' No, Johnny. He had to make a big thing out of it. He had to seem grief-stricken and determined to catch the killer. He just figured I was a safe bet, that it was beyond my powers of deduction to find out he was the one who did it."

St. John raised his glass. "Well done, Sherlock."

"I don't know," Charles answered. "Colonel Larry Coleman cracked mentally the minute he fired point-blank into Ames's chest. He could never let his adored sister know he'd shot the light of her life. His killing Marks and trying to get me killed were the desperate acts of a terrified, demented man."

Donnelly peered up at St. John. "The colonel was sure surprised to see me walk into his office after Belingen, though."

"You were lucky there, you know," said John. "I don't suppose you've been reading *Stars & Stripes?* I'll fill you in. You're getting the Medal of Honor. It was those generals you 'captured' in the hospital that did it."

"Oh? Coleman mentioned something like that, but I didn't take him seriously."

"The fact that, badly wounded, you held the town against overwhelming odds was incidental. But the army weighs things differently, I guess. You were lucky."

Charles sighed. "I wish Buddy'd had a bit of luck. And Terry Kaplan."

"And sweet Isabelle," St. John added sadly. He leaned back in his chair. "You never told me how you knew her, Charles."

"I met her friend. A nurse named Marie."

"Ah, yes. Isabelle told me about Marie. They were childhood friends."

"I promised Marie I'd solve this thing for Isabelle's sake."

"Perhaps she'll take some comfort knowing that the man who killed Isabelle was shot in the heart."

"She already knows. I told her," Charles said, then rose from the table. "I promised her something else. A wartime promise I intend to keep."

John nodded. "The war's ending soon. Then, we'll all be able to count on living and keeping our promises. Now we have our lives in front of us, Charles."

Donnelly fell silent, his mind far away.

EPILOGUE

—◆—

Many years later, after a spectacularly successful law career and ten years as a Federal judge, Charles Donnelly received an appointment to serve on the Supreme Court of the United States. Before the formal White House dinner honoring his appointment, Charles chatted easily with the cabinet members, generals and other dignitaries from the government and from Washington society.

After being seated, the Chief of Staff of the Army commented to several guests, "Judge Donnelly was also a soldier." He said the words proudly, one soldier speaking about another. "A very highly-decorated officer in the Second World War."

"Maybe that's the only reason I'm here," said Donnelly.

The people near enough to hear him laughed.

"Tell me counselor," said the Vice President, "are you going to be a liberal or a conservative justice? Your past rulings don't give us much of a clue. Perhaps that's why you passed through the hearings so quickly."

Charles smiled. "You'll just have to wait and see," he replied. "It depends on how I feel when I get up in the morning. Sometimes I feel liberal and sometimes conservative."

"There," said the Vice President's wife. "I think that puts you in your place." She finished with a curt nod at her husband.

The President of the United States leaned over and said, "Charles, I've been speaking with your lovely wife. She's absolutely captivating. Where did you meet her? At college, I suppose?"

The grey-haired justice smiled and glanced down the immaculately set table at his bride of over thirty years. Her eyes caught the glow of the crystal chandeliers and sparkled with warmth as she returned his smile. To the President, Justice Donnelly said slowly, "No. It was during the war. She was a nurse, you see, and I first met her in a town called Belingen. Belingen on the Main."